Delayed but Not Denied

Teresa B. Howell

Delayed but Not Denied © 2016 Teresa B. Howell
ISBN: 978-0-9977732-3-1

Independent Self-Published through Walking in Victory Int. LLC. P.O. Box 15171 Durham, NC 27704 Printed in the USA
Copyright © 2016 Teresa B. Howell

ISBN: 978-0-9977732-3-1

ACKNOWLEDGMENTS

Thanks to all of my family, friends and readers who support my books. I appreciate all of you more than you will ever know.

SPECIAL DEDICATION

This book is dedicated to my mother, Helen Jean Richardson Ellis, my grandmother Era Bell Ellis, and my uncle Jessie Richardson.
Rest in Heaven.

Stalker-A person who pursues game, prey, or a person stealthily. A person who harasses another person as a former lover, a famous person, etc.
Webster Dictionary

I loved him with all my heart and he belongs to me.

Joy Shackleford

CHAPTER 1–SELINA

While getting dressed for Sunday service, I stumbled across a stack of letters hanging out of my husband's Bible. Desperation was obvious as the writer begged for my husband's affection on every page. With tarnished edges and smeared fingerprints, the jaw-dropping details were explicit, to say the least. Each signature was accented with bright-red lipstick kisses and sprinkled with sweet perfume. The uneasy feelings from my findings brushed upon my heart and shook my soul.

In spite of it all, I threw on my white, loose-fitting dress, combed my hair back into a bun, and made it to church on time. When I entered Ebenezer Baptist, I slid into a pew in the back, next to my mother-in-law. I held my daughter, Jessica, tightly in my arms and rocked. The service moved at a steady pace with the congregation fully engaged. The spirit of the Lord reigned as God's people responded to his presence with dancing. The mass choir sang an upbeat song that buzzed in the middle of my eardrum. The animated choir members banged on tambourines while shuffling their feet to the beat. Their black and white choir robes swished back and forth in unison. The song being sung was one of my favorites. Although the music sounded good, I couldn't focus completely.

He's cheating? I thought as my temper rose slowly to the ceiling. I held curiosity tightly by the fingertips. I wondered what other so-called sanctified woman wanted my husband too. My mind spun in a pool of paranoia each time I looked around at all the beautiful women in the congregation. I wish I could confront all of them one by one someday and ask, *do you want my husband too?* I'm sure my husband's list was long with all the women he probably cheated with. But, I didn't have any proof, with the exception of this one woman's letters. However, I had a gut feeling she wasn't the only one in the midst.

As for the chick who wrote the letters, I was going to step to the wench at the beginning of offering. I tried to keep my cool, but my bad thoughts grew like wild flowers inside my head and became somewhat dangerous.

I was antsy, with continuous illogical thoughts taking over my brain. But in order to keep calm, I continued to rock. I looked down at my baby girl cradled in my arms. She looked just like him. I gazed up at the pulpit. Tall, dark and handsome was an understatement for him. He looked like a Pepsi commercial model ready to take off on the runway. The pride I once had of being his wife dripped away as all the melodrama of suspected church infidelity left me mesmerized.

The music echoed throughout the sanctuary and then the words of the chorus resonated deeply.

This means war…

The choir bounced up and down while singing Pastor Charles Jenkins's hit gospel song "War". I sat upright, trying to feel every beat by tapping my feet and closing my eyes. But, I couldn't concentrate as I pondered over my thoughts. I began to plot my next move quietly. A deep voice inside my head gave explicit instructions.

Walk over to the first pew and speak your peace.

Then the voice became louder and overshadowed my sensibility.

Do it. Embarrass them both in front of the entire congregation.

"Glory, Father," rang out from a woman in my row. It shook me out of my trance. I gazed up at the pulpit again, staring at my husband. To the naked eye, he looked faithful and pure. But, he wasn't. His brown study Bible, where the letters were hidden, remained planted in the center of his hands as he bobbed his head to the beat of the music.

When the song ended, he spat into the microphone, "It is now time for the offering." The musicians started up with the song again as the choir jumped up, following their lead.

"*This means war,*" they all chanted.

"Alright now, church. Now, we all know the program is

subject to change, based upon the movement of the Holy Ghost. So, let's sneak another verse in on the devil. Praise Him while you can, saints!" he shouted.

The audience stood up, clapping to the beat, singing the bridge of the song, "*I plead. I plead the blood.*"

"*Sang,* choir. You sounding good over there!" Bishop yelled into the microphone.

Oh yeah, that's right, he said it's offering time.

That was my cue to open up my can of beat down. I shot straight up out of my seat with my index finger wagging in the air and yelled, "Hold my baby. This means *war.*" Visions of Joseph being with another woman brewed like a bubbling pot of soup all throughout my spirit. A sudden urge to stomp the hell out of anyone standing in my way from getting to her jumped right on my back.

I sped down the aisle, crying angry tears. My footsteps faded forward with power and force. "Help me, Jesus!" I pleaded out loud, as my tears dissolved into my dress.

Not my man, not my husband!

When I reached the front row, I balled my fist ready to strike her as she stood tall, clapping on beat with her fan to the music. "Homewrecker!" I mumbled. I turned in her direction and our eyes immediately met. As soon as I looked deeply into her half-moons, all the rage I had seeped through my toes. I was mute as I tunneled back into reality. My so-called devious plan to strike her came to a screeching halt.

Unfortunately, this husband thief was not a stranger to me and was well-known to the congregation. She wore that same red lipstick that was sealed on the letters. She threw back her head and held a sinister smile. She had a funeral home fan in her hand, which stood between us. It moved from side to side as she looked unbothered, still grooving to the beat of the music. Her big brim hat tilted towards the front of her face with her long weave hanging out of it. Her laced gloves extended down her arms and her skin-tight blouse helped suck in her pudgy stomach. She shot a daring look back, trying to figure out what was my problem as I stood dumbfounded. This was a woman I trusted and loved like a sister. I was devastated to find out she was messing with my husband. A familiar soul that was well known for helping other women find salvation. It was obvious, she was a man-eater who stole my husband's heart. She was also the First Lady of Ebenezer Baptist Church.

CHAPTER 2 – SELINA

I couldn't stop thinking about the sensual statements written in those letters about his manhood as I stood frozen in front of her. Nor could I get over the requests for late-night rendezvous. *How could this be? First Lady Joy and my husband?*

It all made me cringe while pieces of my heart shattered onto the hardwood floor. I remembered all the passion and lust that rested between every sentence. Apparently, she was an undercover freak that enjoyed writing letters to a married man, all along smiling in my face Sunday after Sunday.

Swinging off chandeliers?

Bouncing off bed poles?

Really?

"Is everything okay, Sister Selina?" First Lady Joy reached over with her warm hands and touched my arm. I tried to swallow back tears as I blinked several times, not saying a word.

This is all wrong.

I was supposed to be doing only one thing today and that was reverencing God. Instead, those letters pushed me over the edge and I was ready to exchange blows with the Bishop's wife. It was not my style on how to handle situations. I started to feel like some ghetto chick off one of those reality TV shows. I was bringing drama to God's house and that was not cool. I folded my arms and realized this was not the time nor place to seek revenge. So, I played it all off and said, "I… I guess I came up here for prayer." My eyes were flooded. "I'm in need of a miracle right now."

"Well, come with me, my sister. Let's take it to the altar." She grabbed my hand and led the way landing smack dab in the center of the church. Bishop stood up in the pulpit looking over at us. His face was scrunched with compassion. I'm sure my body language displayed hurt, disappointment, and heartache. But, I'm also sure no one realized it all stemmed from my husband's actions. Bishop pointed his index finger in my direction and spoke loudly into the microphone.

"Sister Selina, God said lay your burdens down before Him. Let Him take care of your every need. I can clearly see the *monkey* you are carrying on your back this morning. Oh, Glory be to God." He waved his hand in the air wildly giving God praise, which sparked another wave of praise from the audience.

I stood at attention in front of the altar like a soldier cadet. First Lady grabbed my hand, whispering, "It's gonna be alright, my sister."

Some nerve.

Nothing was going to be alright until she left my husband alone. My husband and the Bishop stepped down from the pulpit. Bishop leaned in sideways on his three-pronged silver cane, signaling for an usher to bring him the bottle of anointed oil. He then pointed to the congregation. "Now, I know it's not just Sister Selina that needs to lay down some burdens this morning."

"Amen!" the congregation responded.

"For those that need some of this Holy Ghost power, come on up here to this altar and join our sister in prayer."

A group of individuals rushed to the altar surrounding me as I remained standing still. They treated Bishop as if he was God himself. When he said there was power to distribute, he meant the power in stubby fingers that God blessed him with. He moved around slowly, touching the forehead of everyone that participated.

I put my hands over my face, pressing my eyes into my palms, while trying hard to deplete my emotion. I knew this spectacle moment of me getting some form of deliverance was pissing the hell out of my husband. I looked up at him and he rolled his eyes, showing frustration. But, I couldn't turn back now. I needed God.

He inched closer to me with a glance of shame. One would think he was stabbed in the back with a switch blade coated with embarrassment. He gently put his arm around my shoulders and gave me a fake hug of support. He then bent over, whispering in my ear, "Give it to God, baby. He's got you and so do I."

Yeah right.

I huffed, knowing this was all an act to please church folks. Deep down, I'm sure he wished he could've snatched me up and run for the hills. He believed Christian married couples should not expose anything in front of God's people. It wasn't Godly-like, especially when it pertained to him, the associate minister and the Bishop's right-hand man.

Little did he know, he was the reason why I stood in front of the altar inadvertently waiting for a miracle. I wanted him to remove his hands from around my back. Those filthy hands were filled with sin from touching another woman. Just knowing that he laid down with the old coon that stood right beside me made my skin crawl.

First Lady Joy leaned in closer and said, "Yes, listen to your husband, honey. Give it to Him, chile. Give it to Jesus."

Really, God? You're allowing these two hypocrites to pray for me? Are you serious right now?

"Help me, Father!" I yelled in desperation, looking over at

both of them with disgust.

"Give it to him, Sister Selina. Let him have it," Bishop hacked in front of me, slapping me with a spoonful of oil.

"Yes, God, give her what she needs, Father," First Lady Joy screeched in my ear. She then swung my arms high up in the air, forcing me to give God some praise. With her pupils fading, she was acting as if she had personally made a heavenly connection with the Almighty and was guiding my arms to it.

The three of them huddled around, praying away my ailment. I jumped up and down, snatching my hands away and grabbed my elbows. I blocked their voices out, trying hard to focus solely on God as I talked out loud. "Yes, Lord. I need you, Father. Yes, Lord."

Within seconds, I hit the floor, landing on my left side with a thump. I didn't know if it was the Holy Spirit that knocked me down or a slip of the heel. Either way, I laid there, not wanting to get up. Above me, the voices of the three amigos became louder. They amplified their prayers as the crowd joined in with them. Joseph kneeled in front of me. His hand slid up under my torso as he whispered, "Baby, I know postpartum is difficult to deal with, but God will give you the strength you need to get through this." He then scrunched his face and continued. "Now, get up and stop making me look bad."

Postpartum? Really? Does he really think that is what's going on? Mr. Innocent. He never does anything wrong. I'm always the one with a problem that messes up his golden-boy image.

"Oh Lord, heal her right now, God," Bishop pleaded.

I scooted around on the floor, signaling that I was ready to stand to my feet.

"Yes, God. Do it," Joseph responded.

If he says one more word, I'm going to start confessing his sins for him.

He pulled me up and brushed off his black suit. I turned around to face him and gaped at his facial expression. The congregation cheered as if they just witnessed a hurt football player going back in the game. I was going back into the game, alright. I needed to draw up a new defense system in order to defeat all of the women that wanted my man.

"Ain't God good, saints? I said, ain't God good!" Bishop Shackelford screamed in the microphone at the twenty-first century miracle that was just performed. "Church? You see how that man of God stood by his wife while she called on God for her healing? I tell you, that is what good spouses do. A *help meet* is what the Bible calls it." He demonstrated Joseph's walk. "He came down from the pulpit and helped to *meet* her needs. Beautiful. Just beautiful. My Savior."

"Amen!" the church reeled back with excitement.

"We got to pray for marriages all over the world, ain't that right, First Lady Joy?"

She cleared her throat and responded. "Yes, Lord, we shole do."

"We got to pray that there are more marriages like Sister Selina and Minister Joseph's. They set the example for every couple here at Ebenezer." He affectionately eyeballed his wife as she looked away. He then looked back over at us with a gleam of hope in his eyes.

Joseph held my hand tightly, ushering me back to my seat. Once I sat down, he bent over and whispered with a growl, "We need to talk."

"About what?" I asked, without making eye contact.

"What's wrong with you, Selina? Why are you at the altar falling out and carrying on like that this morning?"

I stretched my eyes towards him. "Up there in front of the church, you told me to give it to God, so I did. Now you're angry because it shows that Mr. Perfect is clueless on how to help his wife through her issues. You're such a hypocrite, Joseph. If only you lived by what you preached, then you wouldn't feel as if I'm *embarrassing* you, as you call it. It's not always about you and your image, Joseph."

I waved him away, grabbing the baby from my mother-in-law's arms and looking straight ahead. The congregation stood up clapping with a few "Hallelujahs" and "Thank you, Jesus" All over the room were bright smiles and admiration for our marriage. Joseph smiled back at everyone and shouted, "Thank you, Jesus," while walking back to his seat. Bishop continued to slap oil on the last few members at the altar as the spirit moved all over the building. Before we knew it, the spirit fell down like pouring rain. The oil-sloshing ceremony ended as Bishop walked back to the pulpit yelling into the microphone. "Won't He do it, church? Won't he do it? God is still in the miracle working business, church. My God." Bishop started a two-step dance with his cane leading the way as the music fired up again to compliment his dance. He sparked up several minutes of praise as if he did something spectacular. I wonder would he still be dancing if he knew about the love of his life being a two-bit undercover tramp that just happened to be sleeping with my husband. What goes on in the dark, shall soon come to light.

CHAPTER 3- JOSEPH

I walked back up into the pulpit, subtly giving a hand clap of praise after Selina's stellar performance at the altar. I sat back in my seat, folding my hands in front of me. Why did she always have to be so emotional in front of other people? What was her latest soul-searching fiasco about? What was she dealing with inside her oval-shaped head that I didn't know about?

Embarrassing.

Truth is, my wife has been devoured with sadness since the announcement of our engagement last year. Though I never could pinpoint where the sadness was coming from, I wanted it to go away and be hidden from the public eye. After all, shouldn't a minister's wife be happy in front of the congregation, if nothing else? All that crying and falling out seemed to work my nerves overtime. For some strange reason, she always seems to make me look like a fool.

"Thank you, Jesus," I shouted again, trying to give some form of input to the service without mean mugging the crowd. I started to think back on how things used to be. Before pregnancy, Selina had it all together. *We had* it all together. Our relationship was the epiphany of a perfect marriage and I wanted to make sure it remained that way. But lately, we were two miserable people, co-existing only because we had a child. It was rough, but regardless, we had to keep our image of a strong and loving couple. We couldn't let that die. My daddy taught me early in life to *never let them see you sweat.* I stuck with that motto until this day. It was nobody's business what was going on in my house. Especially not the folks in Ebenezer.

"Glory," I shouted as my hands trembled, thinking about it.

To make matters worse, sex was no longer an option like before. Selina was definitely no longer the vibrant and driven woman I met at Tuskegee University after marriage. I don't know where that person I fell in love with wandered off too, but I wanted her back.

In the beginning of our marriage, Selina would come to church with her head held high, wearing her fierce four-inch heels and strutting around like a prima-donna. Her pearls would be encircled around her neck and her outfit would accentuate her voluptuous curves. I used to like looking at her. There was nothing like sitting in the pulpit, looking down at a beautiful woman that was considered my wife. But now, she came in with her head hanging low, no makeup anywhere to be seen on her face, loose fitting dresses that hid her shape, stockings twisted around her ankles and hair pulled back in a raggedy bun. She performed a complete 180 from all of the things that originally attracted me to her. Once she gave birth, insecurities about her bloated stomach, and stretch marks that expanded from the top of her belly to her thighs were prevalent. But I needed her to snap back to that *beauty is her name* kind of woman I used to know.

Fast.

Her changes caused me to reach back in time, and before I knew it, I was in bed once again with Joy Shackleford, the Bishop's wife. I blinked several times, zooming back into the service, looking into the flap of my Bible. Suddenly, I noticed the letters that Joy put in my Bible were gone. So much for reading snippets of her dirty thoughts before the benediction.

Did Selina find them?

It was obvious. Selina's actions on the altar clearly gave it all away. Especially when she walked up to the front of the church and squared Joy up with balled fists. I was now nervous and hoped my wife wouldn't tell anyone about my surreptitious affair.

Joy winked over at me without shame as she crossed her legs to the right side slowly. She was imploding on my world of marriage easily. Her letters, her flirtatious actions, and her text messages freely expressed her utmost desires. If she had her way, she would've been wifey and not Selina. But, she was of age. We started our relationship during my vulnerable and tender years of life. I was only eighteen still wet behind the ears and she was a spry forty-five.

"Lift your hands up to the Lord and tell Him thank ya," Bishop Shackleford announced. My thought process shifted back into the service. I sat up at attention.

"Thank ya, Father," the congregation reeled.

"One more time for the Holy Ghost."

"Thank ya, Father."

"Let us all have a wonderful week in the Lord. You are now dismissed."

I looked down at Joy as she puckered her lips and then searched the back row for my wife. I was a deer in headlights, thinking about Selina possibly reading the letters. I looked back at Joy again, scanning her body. *Dang*, she was beautiful. Her beauty always seemed to capture me. I stared for a few seconds more and then looked away. She was very easy on the eyes in spite of her age. A true example of the expression *black don't crack*. Her skin was flawless. She didn't have a wrinkle in site. Nor did she look a day over thirty. She was at the age where she could receive senior citizens discounts at the local Golden Corral Restaurant but one couldn't tell.

At age fifty-five, she had it going on. Thick legs, shapely backside, beautiful skin, and an infectious smile. Sometimes I found myself looking over more than twenty times each service. A smile would always emerge from my lips by just thinking about her. I stood up from my seat ready to greet the members.

She winked.

I played it off and looked away.

The truth is, I'd been sleeping with Joy off and on since the night of my engagement party. But once Selina announced that she was pregnant a few months after our wedding, I stopped. I went cold turkey on our affair because I wanted to do the right thing. Not just for myself, but for my unborn child.

Everything was going well and I was being obedient to God's word, until about three weeks ago. Joy made an extra effort to corner me up against a wall in the adult Sunday school classroom. She had a way with her hands and was hard to resist.

I glanced over at her again hoping our eyes would not connect. She was still sitting down with her legs crossed and her long nail extensions tapping on her legs. She looked as if she was waiting around to talk to me. The musicians started playing, "Let the Church Say Amen" by Marvin Winans, giving everyone the cue to exit the building. I watched my wife strap Jessica in her car seat. She didn't even turn around to say goodbye. But she did pull the letters out of her purse and wave them in the air, making sure that I was looking her way. Then, she walked swiftly out of the front door, with Jessica's car seat in one hand

and the letters in the other.

Joy looked around to see if the coast was clear and hauled her slim hips over to my seat.

"Joseph?"

Her 1-900 voice lingered as she stood with her arms folded in front of me.

"What is it, Joy?"

She rolled her neck with annoyance, looking surprised at my response. "Oh, excuse me if I'm bothering you. I saw your wife leave, so I just wanted to check and see if you got the *package* I put in your Bible." She winked.

I looked away, playing dumb and answering with sarcasm, "What package?"

"Oh, you have amnesia now?" She had a piece of peppermint moving around in her mouth, while still trying to sound sexy.

I faced her, eyeballing her chest. "My wife has the letters, so let's end this, shall we?"

"Did she say something?"

"She had them in her hand when she walked out."

She pointed her finger in my face as her fingernail scraped my chin. "Sounds like a personal problem, sweet thing. Hopefully, she will get over it because I need you tonight."

I doubled back at her forwardness. "Excuse me?"

"I've been holding back as you asked, but now it's time to rekindle our love. I tried to respect your wife while she walked around here lopsided and pregnant with your big head baby. But now that the baby is here, I want to see you in your birthday suit tonight around eight pm."

I laughed. "Joy, really?"

"What?" She rolled her neck.

"I'm not meeting you tonight and I'm asking that you just stop writing the letters. I probably should've stopped this a long time ago but I do enjoy reading them."

"I know you do," she snarled.

"Forgive me if I have misled you over the last year, but once I became a married man, I should've buried my feelings for you in the dust. Why don't you let our past go and learn how to love your new husband, Bishop? He seems so sickly and he needs a nurturing and caring wife to help him through his illnesses these days."

"So?" She flailed her fingernails.

"Let's stop this charade of lust we have going on and be the spouses that God called us to be for each of them."

She tapped her foot against the hardwood floor with force. "You're kidding, right? I've been waiting for the moment when I can feel you again. You ain't getting off that easy, sir."

"Let me be honest, Joy. I only asked you to continue

writing the letters because I find the letters to be entertaining. It's not like I want you or anything like that. Don't get it twisted. Our time has passed." I paused, allowing the lie to soak into my tongue.

She doubled back as if she wanted to slap the taste out of my mouth. "Say what? Entertaining? You will *never* stop wanting me, honey. Don't fool yourself. Your response to my hands that day in the Sunday School room proved my point." She narrowed her eyes and crossed her arms.

"Nonsense. Who told you that?" I answered with sarcasm. Although I wanted her, I would never tell her that. Bishop was coming closer and wobbled in our direction.

"You son of a..." she whispered, stepping back while trying to calm herself down. A fake smile was plastered on her face to greet her husband, but her body was tense as she stared back at me.

Bishop walked up, oblivious to the tension between us. Joy frowned and looked back at me with venom in her eyes. She uncrossed her legs with uneasiness and slumped over to the side, leaning on her husband's shoulder.

"Minister Joseph, you ready to deliver the word next Sunday?" He grinned widely.

"I'm always ready. I've learned from the best, Bishop."

He smiled, rearing his head down and smacking his lips on

his wife's cheek. She looked as if she was stung by a poisonous insect.

"Alright, son, I'm counting on you. I need you to bring that fire and brimstone like you always do."

I laughed without adding a comment.

While Bishop remained starry-eyed, waiting for a returned kiss from his wife, Joy flashed a seductive gaze undressing me with her eyes. Her subtle invite didn't go unnoticed as she bounced her eyebrows up and down. She did look beautiful standing there with her skin-tight suit on. Her big brimmed hat made her look like royalty.

Bishop rambled on. "So, we ready for the trunk or treat event next weekend?" We both remained silent, nodding our heads. I ogled down at her voluptuous lips that puckered naturally while she glanced over at my belt buckle.

"We are all set, Bishop."

"Alright, let me get on in this study and handle some paperwork. Enjoy your family today, Minister Joseph. You did a fine job helping your wife reach God this morning." He turned around, making his exit through the side door.

Joy stood there and it was obvious she was not finished with me yet. We both watched Bishop slowly disappear and then she looked back at me. She put her bony finger in my face. "I had you first and I can have you back with the snap of a finger." She demonstrated the snap. "I know what you really want and it ain't that homely little wife of yours." She put her hands on her hips and swished back and forth. I walked off while she was still talking. I wasn't about to create a scene as a few church members lingered around, having conversation with their friends. I wanted to shake her out of mind. But Joy had an everlasting hold on my heart like no other. On my eighteenth birthday, she snatched my virginity from my fragile teenage body.

****

After arriving home to my wife, I put my key in the lock to open the front door. I was greeted instantly as I tried to turn the key. She opened the door and swung it back with force. She eyeballed me for a while before speaking. Then she sputtered with a high-pitched voice. "Not only do I hate that I found your lover's letters, I also hate the fact that I'm pregnant...again." I peered down at her belly and then back into her eyes. I was lost for words.

Another baby?

She turned her back to me and walked up the stairs. When she reached the bedroom, she slammed the bedroom door behind her. This was only confirmation from God that I needed to pay closer attention to my wife and not continue old habits with Joy Shackleford. I stood baffled at the bottom of the stairway with an eerie feeling trickling down my chest.   Joy was the only woman that could engage me into having an affair. But after another child birth announcement, I had to build up the will power needed to end the back and forth.

CHAPTER 4- TIMOTHY

Joseph invited us to his family's Hoover estate after church for dinner. Being an engineer had given him the best life right after college. The Witherspoon's had two living headquarters, a mansion in Hoover on a hillside and a house in suburban Atlanta closer to the infamous Six Flags amusement park. They spent the majority of their time in Atlanta and drove back and forth to church every Sunday. But this particular Sunday, they wanted to spend time in Hoover. Having two, fully furnished homes under the age of thirty was a huge accomplishment for a young African American couple. My wife Maxine and I envied their success.

We were all graduates of Tuskegee University. We hung around one another often. Joseph graduated from the engineering department, I graduated with a Psychology degree, while Maxine and Selina were both Communication majors. We were tight like that in more ways than one. But for me, I was fortunate to have a bond with Selina before our college journey. We grew up together in a small town called Ensley. We carried on as if we were blood relatives at times. I can remember sticking up for her in school as early as the fifth grade. She was a delicate and shy little girl that always wore a flower in her hair, picked from her yard every morning before school. She resembled a china doll and the other little girls were envious over her silky long hair and big beautiful brown eyes. A bashful soul that struggled with advocating for herself. But, I was always there to toughen her up or empower to do great things. Our bond became stronger throughout high school. It was our sophomore year that tragedy struck in Selina's family. I was there for her every step of the way.

"Alright, Selina, what did you burn up this time?" I chuckled, hoping to lighten the mood in the room. It was obvious that there was something going on between the couple. The frequent eye roll exchange, tense body language, and scrunched facial expressions told some of their story. I was uncomfortable to say the least, but I tried to make light of the thick smoke of anger that filled the room.

Selina gave a half grin and answered, "I cooked a pot roast last night. I thought I was doing something fabulous when I added the potatoes and carrots. But it looks like I cooked it too long and it dried out." She glanced back at Joseph, rolling her eyes.

Maxine cleared the lump in her throat as if she was confirming how dry it looked. "Well, it's still edible, right? We can make some gravy and onions to go over it and call it our unique Sunday dinner." She lifted up the stem of her wine glass for a toast with the air as she chuckled at her own commentary.

"You okay, Selina? You look out of it," I said.

Maxine tapped her on the shoulder and said, "That new baby must be wearing you down, girl. Come on, let's go into the kitchen and sift up some gravy that will make this roast pop in our mouths." She grabbed Selina by the hand and they both walked into the kitchen to conjure up something special. The dried-out cow sat in front of us screaming for help.

I was curious as to what was going on between the two of them and didn't hesitate to ask. "What's good, bro?" I turned to him, waiting for him to dish out the 411. It seemed as if something serious was causing such an uncomfortable environment, because he looked just as exhausted as Selina.

He slumped over the table with grief in his eyes. "Everything is falling apart, bruh."

"How so?"

"Selina is pregnant again and Joy won't go away."

"Congrats on the new bambino. But wait, you've been getting busy with Joy again?"

"Nah, just a little flirting, a little touching here and there. Nothing serious."

"A little touching? Why aren't you touching on your wife,

dog?"

"Man, didn't I just say my wife was pregnant again? It's obvious that if she's knocked up, a lot of touching has been going on." He gave a long sigh.

"Then why is Joy still in the picture?"

"She keeps writing me letters, flirts often, calls, sends text messages. I guess she feels the longer she can keep my attention, the better chances she has of getting me in bed."

"Does Selina know about this?"

"She knows about the letters, that's it. She found them this morning in my Bible."

"I see Joy is still pulling you by your—"

He panicked, slapping his hands down on the table. "Shhh, they can hear you in the kitchen, man."

"Oh my bad. Well, why do you keep playing this game with her? It's obvious you must like the attention."

He gave a sly grin. "I'm not going to lie, bro. I enjoy it at times."

Since Maxine and I had dried up in the bedroom department, I was getting excited about his double life and wanted to know more information. "What did the letters say?" My voice lowered, now feeling ashamed that I asked.

"The usual. You know, the kinky stuff."

"Wait, she hasn't been married to Bishop for three months

and she coming at you like that?"

His eyes were now lower than mine. "Habit, I guess."

"Huh I see." My eyes rose.

"Yeah, bruh. We got history."

"I guess all the new circumstances of being a wife didn't change her heart for you, huh?"

"Apparently not. They weren't even married for a week when she called me to tell me that she missed me."

"Sounds like some *Cougar* love." I burst into laughter.

Joseph's hands rubbed across the tablecloth as he leaned in closer threatening to punch me in the arm. "Shut up. What should I do, bruh?"

"You can't control Joy's actions, but you can control your own. Stop dealing with her. Leave her in the past before someone gets hurt."

"Joy ain't giving up that easy, man. She was my first and she loves throwing that fact in my face daily."

"Say what?" I was startled by the news.

"You heard me, bruh. I never shared that with you while we were kicking it at school. So, be sure to take that to the grave with you. Joy used to be heavy on alcohol back then. She used to get really drunk and then come and find me. Once we got together on a serious note, she slowed down on all that drinking because I helped her get through it. That made her want me even more."

"Mercy." I winced.

"Man, why you so loud? If you don't lower your voice up in here." His face was turning bluish green as he kept looking back at the kitchen door.

Within seconds, the door to the kitchen swung open. "Here it is…the ultimate supreme Sunday dinner. The gravy was made by yours truly and my cooking sister, Maxine." Selina placed it on the table. As they both gave a bow, she said, "How does it look?" We all stared down into the ceramic bowl of gravy with onions swimming on top.

"Looks good to me," I responded. It's not like I knew what roast gravy was supposed to look like since Maxine didn't cook at home. I was now worried about my friend. Although she tried to play it off, her eyes were filled with darkness. She looked just like that little girl I once knew who found her mother and father dead on the living room floor. I knew what that look meant as I prayed silently. If Joseph didn't get himself together soon, it was going to be difficult to keep Selina around. Her heart was hardened after losing her parents. I thought hooking her up with Joseph would make her happy again. But as I looked across the table, I could feel her spirit quickening. She was broken inside and what Joseph didn't realize is that it would be hard to bring love back once lost. If she went back into her old state of mind, it would mean trouble for the once happy couple. If he didn't get himself together, she would run from it all. That was her pattern…running from her problems.

I didn't want my sister suffering inside due to a woman that didn't have morals about commitment. I also didn't want Joseph to lose his wife. They were beautiful together. I was going to try my best to intervene and help my brother remain faithful. But I also wanted to help my sister continue to flow love in and out of her damaged heart.

We gathered hands as Joseph blessed the food.

"Yes, this looks delicious." I rubbed my hands together anticipating the savory taste of southern cooking. Needless to say, the gravy didn't help the roast at all. We all sat in silence chewing down hard with fake smiles, pretending to enjoy our overcooked Sunday dinner.

CHAPTER 5- JOY

6 months later...

"Is he dead yet?" I felt myself frowning after I released those words. My husband laid in a bulky hospital bed full of fever. I didn't mean to sound so cold, but the words shot out of my mouth like rising flames. It was unfortunate, but he had a massive heart attack. I was tired of the hospital scene as he was always sick. It hadn't even been a year into our marriage yet, and I was already tired of being his first lady.

I anxiously awaited death to come, hoping that my imaginary chains from marriage would be released off my feet. What a big mistake I made. Marrying the Bishop shouldn't have happened. I knew doggone well that I wasn't over Joseph, but greed and power helped me make the decision to say, "I do."

The ICU section of the hospital was gloomy, cold, and full of dim lighting. It was a place where the continuation of life wasn't promised. His breathing, heartbeat, and brain activity were evaluated minute by minute. I watched through a glass wall as tubes ran in and out of Michael's nose and mouth. The sad part is since his last heart attack, I kept the funeral home on speed-dial. The outline of his obituary was also created, just in case.

He was in bad shape. His lips were chalky white, face bloated, his feet reflected an orange tinge of color, and an off-white cloth mask covered his mouth. I thought back to how it all happened.

Late evening, Michael's oldest son, Robert from his previous marriage found him unresponsive on the porcelain kitchen floor. "Oh my God." When I heard his son yell while upstairs in our townhome, I rushed down to see what the commotion was all about. I bit my lip as he laid in the middle of the floor, stiff and non-responsive. "What's going on?"

His children's eyes pierced into my backside, as they waited for me to make a move. "Everyone step back. I got this." My role as a caring and concerned wife went over well as I rushed to the telephone on the kitchen wall and dialed 911. "Please hurry. My husband is on the floor unresponsive. Please send someone soon." Within minutes, Bishop was taken to the county hospital in Birmingham. He was rushed in, and shortly after, they performed surgery. Two stents were added to his heart and he was given the opportunity to live a little while longer.

I looked over at him with disgust, wondering why I continued to play this game as if I cared. As the machines attached to him pinged loud noises, I couldn't help but to think about how he resembled a fried discolored vegetable, smothered in margarine, laying there. There was an ill feeling about my future in the pit of my stomach as the hospital aroma hit my nostrils sideways. I started to feel bad about my situation, as being with a sickly man was not my plan. I once thought I loved him. But, I didn't. Truth is, I loved Joseph.

Joseph made it clear right after graduating from college that we couldn't be together, no matter how deep the love. We both knew our drastic age differences wouldn't be pleasing to church folks. I was twenty-seven years his senior and with his all American-boy reputation around town, he wasn't about to take any chances of messing that up. The town of Hoover, along with Ebenezer Baptist Church, loved Joseph just as much as I did. He was close to seven feet tall, dark and handsome. He had charisma and an infectious laugh that could warm all hearts. He was caring and loved to support God's people, no matter what the circumstance. He helped me put down the bottle years ago and I helped him experience the right way to love. He was mostly known in the community for helping his high school team win the state football championship. The people of Hoover considered him a football legend and the ladies were always in hot pursuit for his attention.

After graduating from Tuskegee University, he brought his half-Asian, half-black little homely wife to the church. During

Sunday School one Sunday, he announced that he was getting married and purchasing a home in Atlanta. But he would never leave Ebenezer, no matter the distance, because it was *home*.

I wanted to use every waking opportunity I could get to make him love me again. Time was passing us by and being married to the Bishop didn't mean a hill of beans to me. Joseph was her husband, only on paper. When it came to the heart, he belonged to me. One day, I was going to make her realize that fact.

CHAPTER 6 JOY

Joseph walked in the ICU hurriedly. When he laid eyes on Bishop, he stopped dead in his tracks with shock smeared across his face. Our eyes met. He turned away and looked back at Bishop lying in the hospital bed.

"Good to see you, Minister Joseph." I nodded.

He nodded back.

A tinge of euphoria showered my heart as he stood there quietly.

Suddenly, he spoke, "Is he... Is he going to make it?" He put his hand over his mouth as he observed.

I jumped up from my seat, grabbing his hand with an attempt of leading him down the hallway to gain a kiss or two. "Let's talk outside, I don't want anyone to disturb us."

He jerked his hand away, giving me a jarring stare.

I looked back, grabbing his arm again with force. "Didn't you hear me?"

"I'm not going anywhere with you, Joy."

I was puzzled by his level of rejection. He had his moments of pushing me away, but never like this. This would have been a prime opportunity to touch him all over and make him forget about all of his troubles.

"Why do you go to great lengths to avoid me now, Joseph?"

His head fell back as if it seemed to be a ridiculous question. "Joy, I told you a few months ago that I didn't want you writing letters anymore and that I needed you to leave me alone. My wife is expecting again and I need to focus on my family, not your raunchy letters or those octopus hands of yours. It's timeout for playing games. It's time to get serious with God."

I ignored his spiritual enlightenment. "Do you think of me at all, Joseph? I know you love me."

He blinked, answering harshly, "No." He placed his fingers on the glass.

"Once upon a time, we were in love. You did once love me, right? Or was that a figment of my imagination?"

He shrugged his shoulders nonchalantly. "Yes, once. But I'm happily married now and for some reason you seem to keep trying to destroy my happiness."

"Lies," I interjected while picking my fingernails.

He looked at me with sincerity in his eyes. "What we had is the past. Let it go, Joy." The volume of his voice went up and down due to his trembling lips. He looked around annoyed as if it hurt him to say those words.

He spat the truth, but that wasn't what I wanted to hear. I knew he was trying hard to be a good husband over the past few months. That's why ruining his happiness became my number-one goal. She didn't deserve him. I did.

"Word on the street is you're now vocalizing how you feel about me to other people. You've never did that before. Is the sting of rejection making you chatty now?"

I gave a cold look.

"I need you to keep my name out of your mouth."

I folded my arms in defense. "Nonsense. I don't talk about our past relationship to anyone but God." I held my breath, hoping that the lie I told wouldn't burn through my tongue.

Kimberly…

It was now apparent that my hair stylist, Kimberly, had the biggest mouth in Hoover, Alabama. I told her all of my dirty secrets a few weeks ago but I had no idea that she would share it with anyone else. Silly me, I should've known giving juicy gossip about how the first lady got her groove back would be too tempting for anyone to keep to themselves.

He looked over with disbelief. "Yeah, whatever. You can stop lying to me. People talk."

His abrasive tone sunk me deep into an oblivion of shame. I had no intentions on hurting him and I knew how he was a private person that despised gossip. Kimberly's diarrhea of the mouth probably messed up any chance I had of getting him back. He didn't like taking chances of having a tarnished reputation in the church. I knew he was worried because his sparkling, golden boy image was not going to carry out until his dying day as anticipated.

I opened my arms to hug him, knowing the impact my big mouth had caused. I had to come clean with him. "Please don't hate me. Okay, I made a mistake. I did share it with someone. I know how you hate stuff like that. But I need you to know, I love you, Joseph. Let's sit down and talk this out."

He waved me away with his hands. "Not happening, Joy. I only talk things out with the woman that matters, my wife. You are no longer my concern."

That cut like a knife.

His eyes shunned me, making me feel worse than I was already feeling. I cleared my throat trying to be sincere. "Alright, let's change the subject. We are both here for Bishop, right? So, shall we pray for him together?" I reached out to grab his hand, waiting for him to grab mine. Suddenly, I was engulfed with the scent of his cologne. It made love to my nose. I imagined myself making him bend down so I could rub his closely shaven head. I wanted to caress him and put my breasts up against his chest—just like we used to do. I admired his perfect body as I waited a few more seconds for him to join my hands in prayer. My eyes continued to wander as he sparked several flames of passion inside of me. I was reminded over and over of the good old days.

I continued to wait for a response.

He looked stunning in his tailored black suit with a red bow tie. His matching handkerchief hung out of his left pocket as his hands were still touching the glass wall.

"I'd rather pray by myself, thank you." He looked over, gesturing his point by throwing quotation marks in the air.

"Please. Let's not do this, Joseph. We have too much time and energy invested in one another. That one-year marriage you got going on doesn't have anything on what we have shared. Don't you want that feeling back again? Don't you want me in your arms? Your wife is just a baby-making machine and I'm sure you ain't getting none on the regular either. Let me love you, Joseph."

He blew his breath. "Anyway, I'm here for Bishop and Bishop only. You are not the one on my radar."

"What?" If I could have strangled him to death, I would have. What a crass thing to say after all those years of love and support we gave one another. I guess he thought he was better than me, now that he had his little mixed trophy wife on his arm. I wasn't going out like this. He was going to love me again, whether he liked it or not.

"What happened to him? Another heart attack?"

"Yes," I moaned.

"I thought he was doing better." His eyes filled with shock and hurt.

"Yeah, well, he's not."

A stunned expression covered his face. He put one finger up signaling me to hush as he tried to take it all in giving a long exhale. I gave him a few minutes to swallow and process it all. The two of them were close and Bishop treated him like a son. He seemed disheveled as he smoothed his hands down his face.

We traded a glance again as he quickly jolted his eyes in the other direction. I wanted him to look me dead in my face, but he wouldn't. I wanted him to see the pain he was causing in my eyes by pushing me away. I wanted him to know by my demeanor that I couldn't live without him. But instead, he continued to look in the other direction.

"I hope he makes it, because I'm not cut out to be the pastor at Ebenezer."

I doubled back. "Well, who is?"

He shook his head. "Heck, aren't you the backup plan?"

I hissed.

"Oh that's right, I forgot, maybe if you stop focusing on me, you'll be able to put your undeserving minister's license to better use."

I shuddered. "Is that jealousy or hate I hear in your voice?"

"Whatever."

"Do you remember that night at the hotel, right after your engagement party? Let me refresh your memory on how good that night was for the both of us. Since you want to play me like I was some sort of cheap thrill. I didn't hear you talk like this that night. All I heard was 'Oh Joy, baby, please, oh that feels so good.'"

He flashed a flutter of nervousness with his hands. "Stop talking."

"That night after you placed that big rock on Selina's finger and gave her that big grandiose dinner, with the entire church oohing and aahhing at your fake love affair, guess what you wanted for dessert? *Me*." I pushed my finger, pricking him in his chest.

My feathers were completely ruffled by his snarling commentary.

I paused, took a deep breath and said, "I can't live without you, Joseph."

"If you say so." He gave a dismissive sigh. His caved in eyebrows turned inward like the grinch that stole Christmas. I didn't understand how he could be so mean to me. I couldn't understand why he pretended like he didn't love me, after all we had been through together. I brushed up against his arm. I couldn't resist taunting and teasing him. His eyes became vacant. I rubbed his biceps gently. His athletic build thrilled me. I wanted him. Boy, did I want him. His hot spots were cataloged in my heart and I was ready to explore them right there in the middle of the hospital room floor, if he allowed me to.

He looked down at me with disgust and said, "*Really,* Joy?"

"Don't you want me like I want yo—"

He stopped me mid-sentence, as his chest swelled up. I was in la-la land. The lust bug had stung me in my left ovary and I couldn't help myself.

He cleared his throat, pulling away. "I gotta go." His voice cracked as if he felt something from my touch. He dropped his hands to his side trying to gain composure. "Call me if Bishop wakes up any time soon. I have nothing else to say to you, Joy."

I paused, catching my breath and swallowing hard, pushing the lust bug off of me. "Okay. I understand. I love you."

He nodded gravely. "Don't you ever say that out loud again. Keep that between you and God." He looked back at Bishop as if he could hear us.

I smoothed my hands down my thighs. "You don't want this, Joseph?" I pushed up my cleavage with the tip of my palm, hoping he would admire my silicone breasts that Kim Kardashian would be envious of.

His feet shuffled in front of him as he stepped forward.

"Bye, Joy. You need to get a life," he mumbled.

Within seconds, he disappeared down the hallway. It was the same way he disappeared out of my life, by moving straight ahead without looking back. His maid service that he called wife stole all of my joy.

I should've been his wife. I should be the one he holds at night.

I rushed to the bathroom feeling so emotional. I had to freshen up in order to shake these feelings. I was hotter than a pan of scalding hot fish grease after being that close to him. Nothing seemed to stop the feelings that controlled me.

The role played of being a saved and sanctified Bishop's wife had left the building. My panties were steamed and my cinematic imagination of the two of us together was in full effect. I wanted Joseph back. Back in my arms, back in my bedroom, back in my life. I didn't know how to make that happen, but I was surely going to keep trying.

CHAPTER 7- SELINA

Falling in love with Joseph started off like a magical love story that could be seen on Netflix. It was my first real experience with loving a man. I was elated to find someone with charm, wit, and gentleman-like characteristics such as him. He also had a sex appeal like no other. But, I knew when I met him that our relationship was going to be challenging, due to his popularity. I eventually agreed to take on that challenge and I was elated when I became his wife.

The memories of my father killing my mother over infidelity lingered. Instead of looking at marriage as a bad thing based upon that experience, I strived for a perfect marriage. Clearly, my dad turning the gun on himself expressed to the world that there is no such thing as a perfect marriage. But, I still believed. I still had hope and I wanted a special union for us.

After joining Ebenezer, I realized it was important to Joseph that we remain perfect at all times. In spite of women flashing smirks or engaging in long conversations with him, I was supposed to remain understanding and supportive. I even endured the late-night phone calls from women that wanted to "talk" about getting closer to God with him. But, I kept my cool at all times and I was committed to making our *image* sparkle brightly. I was also committed to showing the world that our marriage could overcome any obstacle. Even if infidelity stepped up at my front door, we would make it. That's what I believed until it actually happened.

Our first son, Josiah, was born a few months ago. Another black male that needed to learn the quality of being committed to one woman. I prayed he would grow up to be a man with morals and values that would withstand temptation. I also prayed he wouldn't grow up caring about what church people thought. I wanted him to follow God's will and not the will of church membership. I didn't want him perpetrating like we were doing. I wanted him to level up in God and make his future wife happy.

******

The night of Bishop's heart attack, Joseph called and asked if I could meet him at the hospital. I was still in Hoover with the kids at their grandparents' house and it wouldn't be hard to get away for a moment or two. Joseph assumed he would be at the hospital for a while and wanted me by his side. I didn't know if it was because he needed my support, or if he wanted me to be his shield and sword against Joy. Either way, I knew

Bishop being ill would take a toll on him. I also knew Joy would be somewhere in the midst. On this day, she wasn't going to get that chance to pant and coo over my man. I was going to be standing right there with him through this sorrowful time.

When I walked into the ICU area, I didn't see anyone in sight. I heard a faint voice across the room. "Sister Selina. Welcome. Thank you for coming to check on Bishop," Joy greeted with a snarl.

I looked around for my husband and asked, "Joseph told me to meet him here. Where is he?"

She scoffed, rubbing her hands together. "Your husband just left a few minutes ago. I guess Bishop wasn't his main concern after all."

Lots of things raced through my mind as I looked around trying to figure out what to do or say next.

"You know, Selina, it took me awhile but I finally figured out why you came up to me that Sunday morning wanting prayer."

"Oh yeah?" I answered self-consciously, squinting my eyes.

"Well, I realized it wasn't prayer you were looking for at all. I think you had something you wanted to say to me."

I shrugged my shoulders. "Maybe."

"Did you have something on your mind, darling? I'm all ears now, so what was it?" She waved her long fingernails awaiting my response. I turned around, slowly pivoting my feet in her direction. It was now a grand opportunity to set the record straight. I blurted out words quickly after moving closer. "Why, as a matter of fact, I did have something to say, First Lady."

She grinned with an anticipated look.

I spoke frantically as I was anxious to get it all out. While pointing at her, I screeched with emphasis, "Stay the hell away from my husband!"

She chuckled as her body shook up and down, unmoved by my loud outburst. She made a few steps forward charging towards me and said, "Or else what?"

I stood tall, unflinching. "Or else, he will be the last husband you come after."

Her eyes bucked out of her head as her fingers flailed wildly. "I beg your pardon. Are you threatening me, Sister Selina?"

"You heard what I said. The only person in this room that might be hard of hearing right now is Bishop." I looked over at Bishop lying still with machines attached and then back at her. "If you come for my husband again with your filthy letters, flirtatious glares, or flaunting your *hoeish* behind in his face, we are going to have some serious problems."

Her face turned red as her yellow complexion became

orange covered with sweat. Her voice clipped. "For your information, I taught your husband everything he knows about how to please a woman. You are enjoying him every night based upon my fabulous training. You should be thanking me for the free lessons he's received over the years to please your scrawny behind."

Her words were a painful reminder that they had been together, which sparked a new-found sting in my fist. "You're just jealous that you can't have him." I stepped to her face and slowly released my words. "You envy me, don't you?" I hissed, while eyeballing her up and down.

She wagged a finger in my face. "Let me say this, young lady...if I want him, I can easily have him." She then clasped her hands together, showing that she was trying to keep her composure.

My hands vibrated. I was trying so hard to calm down. "Try me if you want to. I *repeat*. Stay away from my husband, hussy." I took a deep breath. I hadn't been that mean to anyone in my entire life. Name calling wasn't my thing, but my words echoing throughout the room made me feel validated. He was my man and I was the boss in this situation.

I made sure she could feel my words that clearly explained, *I'm not the one.* I knew by the way of my delivery, the raw edge of my tone could be understood amongst every religion, faith, and language. However, I wasn't finished yet. "And guess what? This threat doesn't come with an expiration date." Veins began to pop out of her forehead. I wasn't sticking around to wait for a response, but I was determined to have the last and final words in the matter. I swirled around with confidence in my tight jeans, with my hands on my hips and walked out. It was now praying time, because after giving Joy Shackleford the business, there was no doubt that she would push her cougar claws out to get what she wanted.

Delayed but Not Denied

CHAPTER 8 - JOY

Two weeks later...

I arrived at the hospital bright and early that morning. Michael had been moved to another section of the hospital based on his improvement. A transitory flash hit me concerning Selina's appearance a few weeks ago at the hospital. Her words ignited me to get my man far away from her. I had several tactics in mind on how to keep Joseph's attention. I didn't care what anyone thought if it all came out in the open. I loved him. I *really* loved him.

Now that I'd decided to leave Michael once he recovered, I was all about getting my *real* man back. Being a first lady was a true drag as I pretended to be something I was not for way too long. I was tired of living a lie. I didn't like Michael breathing on me, let alone touching me like normal couples would do. I was totally turned off after the first week of marriage. It wasn't his fault in the matter, but I wish I could turn back the hands of time. Along with all the other things I didn't like about him, having sex with him was a joke. He was too sickly to do anything to please me. I wasn't aware of that in the beginning and settled, despite my strong cravings for sexual pleasure.

Why was I still with this man?

Why did I marry him anyway?

What in the hell was I thinking?

I gazed back at Michael and then at my watch, hoping I could escape from this visit as soon as possible.

"*Jo…*" he mumbled, with several coughs behind his words.

I jerked my neck in his direction surprised at his ability to speak.

"I'm here," I responded flatly, leaning in closer to hear him.

He gave a crooked smile and opened his eyes slowly.

"How are you feeling?" I asked.

Being cordial, not that I cared.

He tried to mouth a few sounds but nothing came out. I gazed over and shook my head as he attempted again while grabbing the sheet on the bed.

"Ccccccchhhh?"

Church? I should've known he would ask about that doggone church before anything else.

"Church?"

He tried to move his head up and down to deliver a subtle nod of confirmation.

"I'm sure the church will remain in tip-top shape until you return. Joseph is doing a fine job with the ministry." I patted his hand, giving a wide grin.

A man with a blue uniform came into the room with a tray of food and placed it on the side of the bed. The aroma of the anticipated hearty meal made my stomach gurgle. I realized I hadn't had breakfast and hoped there would be enough for the two of us to share. I removed the yellow covering, frowning up at the bland food selection. Everything on the plate looked watery, strained, or overcooked. A cup of water was put on the side, which by the looks of it, would be needed to wash down the mess of a meal. Everything looked disgusting.

He cracked a half loving grin with his eyes glossed over while malicious thoughts entered my mind. Thoughts such as how to manipulate Joseph into loving me. Deeper thoughts on how I could meet with Selina and remove her from our storyline. Angry thoughts on how to end Michael's life as he laid in the bed still feeble and shriveled up. The love for Joseph was taking me to unfamiliar places and making me crazy. But I wanted him and now I was flooded with *by all means necessary* thoughts.

I once watched a Showtime special where a man killed his wife with a poisonous berry plant. I found that to be a clever way of getting rid of someone and it hovered in the back of my mind. Could I possibly get up the nerve to do something like that to Michael in order to escape this marriage?

Ugly thoughts.

Sinful thoughts.

I had no outlet to get rid of the images in my mind. I felt like putting my hands up to my ears and screaming. I wanted to release these thoughts immediately. A bottle of Scotch would be a wonderful tool to help me with my problem. It used to work well for me years ago when it came to releasing bad thoughts.

As my brain churned, I picked up the spoon on the tray, dabbed it in the plate of food and shoved it into Michael's mouth. I moved closer to the bed as my thoughts became words. I whispered softly into his ear, "Don't you want help with getting to the golden gates, baby? Aren't you tired of being bogged down in here like this?"

His weak smile turned into a frown as he looked surprised at my words. I continued to spoon his food aggressively into his mouth. "Blink three times if you want me to help you with this. No need to keep suffering, babe. After all, when you get out of here, I'm not going to want you anyway."

A tear dropped from his eye and rolled down his face.

I wasn't fazed as I continued to torture him with my abrasive talk. "What can you do for me? You're washed up, limp, and of no use." I moved the spoon away and waited for several minutes. I was hoping to get those three blinks of confirmation. But instead, he stared right through me as if I was a glass sculpture, giving a mystified daze.

I smacked my lips and continued. "Doctors say you might be permanently paralyzed after this one. The truth is, I didn't sign up for this type of lifestyle. I only married you for your money and notoriety. Never loved you, you know."

His eyes filled with water as disappointment and hurt poured out of his pupils and onto his hospital gown.

I pointed the spoon straight up ignoring his pain. "I hear there's this white baneberry that gives an immediate sedative effect. After eating several of them, it eventually leads to death. And guess what? The first thing it attacks is the heart. Perfect way to leave this earth since your heart is already damaged." I nodded confirming how well it would work. "It would be the perfect antidote to set your soul free, honey. Wouldn't you like that? The church wouldn't miss you and neither would I."

His face turned red as he attempted to mumble.

I cuffed my hand behind my ear and asked, "What are you trying to say, honey?" I bent over, putting my ear close to his lips for a better understanding. "Say it louder, dear. I can't hear you."

"D..." he blurted.

"What's that?"

His face puffed up as his mouth trembled. He gave out a big gasp and said, "Devvvvilll." He then exhaled deeply as his chest slumped down.

"Devil?"

He let out a loud grunt to confirm that was the word he wanted to share with me. Before I realized it, I was shoving the spoon deep down into his throat. I lost control and instantly wanted to stop him from breathing. But something inside me pulled the spoon back out of his mouth as he gasped for air.

He moaned in pain.

"I got your devil. Since you won't take me up on my proposition, the nursing home will be your next stop."

A bitter expression swept across his face. He looked as if he just lost his best friend.

I scooted back in my chair, trying my best to gain control. But, I just couldn't stop talking. I wanted him to know how I really felt about the matter. "It's not my job to take care of your gravely ill behind. Let your snotty nose children from your first wife do that for you." I cringed while thinking about the responsibilities I would inherit if he came home after this attack. "I want to be free, Michael. I want to live my life like it's golden. I want to drink, smoke, and lay up as long as I can with whomever I want. Yes, I know it sounds crass. But, I'm tired of being your goody-goody wife."

He closed his eyes and turned his head to the side. I knew I had gotten to him. That was the plan.

"And by the way, while I'm clearing the air, I don't love you either. I'm sure you could pick up on that by now. You will suffer tremendously once you leave this hospital, believe that."

"D…devvvilll!" He blurted clearly with his eyes still closed as his face filled with disgust.

I pacified the behavior with a luscious smile. "Okay, I will be your devil then since you insist. I know what I'm saying right now is probably considered evil, hateful, and spiteful especially in the eyes of a bishop. But this marriage was dead before it even got started."

I followed his eyes to the window. The shade was up and there was no sunlight shining in. It was as if dark clouds rushed across the sky and instantly hid the light. It depicted the full story of my life. Light to darkness without my Joseph.

I threw the spoon down on the floor with disgust thinking about it. If only I had a handful of those poisonous berries to push into Michael's mouth right about now. Something had to give so I could be with my heart, Joseph Witherspoon.

CHAPTER 9- JOSEPH

Sunday evening, I hung around after service helping Timothy lock up the church. I was planning to stop by the hospital afterwards to check on Bishop. However, I had to pack up and get back to Atlanta before it got too late. This particular month me and my family stayed in the Atlanta home so I could catch up with work. Between work duties, husband duties, daddy duties, and church duties, I was exhausted.

"You're still worried about Bishop, huh?" Timothy inquired.

"That along with other things."

"You've been looking out of it all night. Your emotions are all down your sleeves. I'm sure Joy is still at it, too, huh."

"Yeah. It's been a crazy week."

"Yeah, bruh. No hallelujahs from you this evening, that's for sure."

I tried to convince myself over and over again that everything was going to be alright, but it wasn't working.

"Not having Bishop around is difficult. Without him, there is no one here to tame her. What am I gonna do?"

"Bishop will come out of this and hopefully he will get her to act right. You wait and see."

I held my face, feeling overwhelmed. "So much is going on right now."

He walked with me to the back of the church in step. "What else is it?"

"I just want my marriage to be the way it used to be. Selina and this post-partum mess isn't helping either. Has she reached out to you lately?"

"A few days ago."

"She won't talk to me so I figured she would at least talk to you. Can you talk to her?"

"Yeah but talking to her won't stop her paranoia about other women in your face. She told me how it is every Sunday. That's probably taking a toll on her along with the babies."

"See, that's the stuff I'm talking about. Why does she think like that? I don't pay those other women any mind. All of this is making my head hurt." I rubbed my temple.

"So basically, Selina needs time to heal from the last time you hurt her. It also looks like all this nonsense going on with these other women takes her backwards not forward in your marriage. As for Joy, you two got it bad for one another and don't even know it."

"Say what?" I lifted my head up quickly. "I don't have it

bad for anyone but my wife."

"The reality is, she helped you find your manhood and you helped her put down the bottle."

I wiped my forehead clean. "So?"

"So, the two of you will always be attached in some form. It was tit for tat."

"I don't believe that's true, bruh."

"Well, it's true for her, that's why she won't let go." He patted me on the shoulder. "Plus, she's probably going through a midlife crisis or menopause. She is old, you know."

We both laughed in unison.

"I honestly don't pay her any mind."

"I hear you talking." He looked back with a skeptical stare. "Do you tell Selina every time Joy is in hot pursuit?" he asked.

"I didn't used to until she found those letters in my bible. With the roller coaster of emotions she was having, I had to."

"How did she get to them anyway?"

"Apparently, she saw them sticking out of my Bible when I laid it on the bookshelf in the living room."

"You don't say." He laughed loudly. "You slipping."

I shrugged my shoulders.

"Sounds like Joy is now on a safari hunt for her tiger. Ole cougar," he said sarcastically.

I didn't say a word as Timothy squinted reading my facial

expression. He put his hand on his chin. "I'm on your side, bro, but without Bishop in place, she is going to run wild until you're captured. The communication and letters should've ended years ago."

I shook my head in disgust. "Why can't she just love the one she's with and leave me alone?"

"She can't, Negro, because she is still in love with *you*! What part are we missing here?"

I folded my arms, walking out the door.

Timothy followed behind me and continued. "Yooo, listen. All I'm saying is be careful, dude. I watched a documentary about a woman going crazy over an ex. In the end, she went postal on his entire family. For a woman to chase you this long without caring about her actions and who gets hurt in the process sounds dangerous." He patted me on the back as if he knew something that I didn't.

I laughed, trying to play it off. "Really? That's how you see it?"

"Bruh, you need to pay attention, that's all I'm saying. You don't know what she is capable of."

"I'm not worried."

He pulled the back door towards him and started singing. "It's a thin line between love and hate." Or should I be singing something current like 'Boo'd up' to explain your situation?" he chuckled. "And don't act like you wasn't rushing home from college every weekend to be with Joy, before I hooked you up with Selina. This ain't all on her. You had deep feelings for her, too."

I dismissed his observation by waving my hand. "I was young and excited to be with an older woman, that's all. She needs to get a grip."

He looked up with another skeptic blink. "Yes, she really does because when it's all said and done, Selina just isn't in a good head space right now to be dealing with all of this. I want to help both of you through this, because I know how detrimental this could be for Selina. I'm a living witness of how badly Selina suffered from the loss of her parents. She's starting to have that same look she did way back then. So now I'm asking you to ensure her happiness at all cost. What can I do to help?"

I grunted giving a serious face. "If you can keep Joy away from me, maybe we can all live happily ever after."

"You ain't said nothing but a word, bruh. I got you." I winked for confirmation.

CHAPTER 10- TIMOTHY

Joseph tried to convince himself that he was strong enough to resist Joy by simply ignoring her. Who was he kidding? Did he forget that I lived through several years of not only this particular love triangle but also a few more that involved him and other women? There was something still hot and heavy between the two of them, even if he didn't want to come to grips with it. But, he was playing the sanctified husband role these days and he played it well. I was hoping for the sake of Selina's happiness that his feelings for Joy Shackleford were pushed in the Pandora 's Box of his mind.

I stood in my living room swirling my ice in my cup, thinking about it all. Maxine sat quietly on the sofa staring into space as she took her microbraids out of her hair. I guess in a sense our relationship was similar to the Witherspoons. We hadn't been happy in a while. We just didn't talk about it or make it our focal point.

While I tried not to be the overprotective big brother always thinking about Selina's well-being, I couldn't help myself. Maxine accused me once of having more than just brotherly love for Selina. That wasn't the case. Trying to protect her was now habit. Maxine and Selina were like salt and pepper when it came to personalities. The difference between her and Selina was that Maxine was extremely vocal and never held back on how she felt. Whereas, it took a lot to get Selina to talk about how she was feeling without shedding tears. Lately, Maxine had a lot to say about Selina and Joseph's situation as she watched the distance between them unfold. I guess I didn't help either as I was always talking about it. I had a sense of guilt for introducing the two of them. I had no idea Joseph had feelings for Joy the way he did, even if he didn't acknowledge them. It was obvious he felt something for her. I hated the fact that I put Selina in such a predicament that would push her back into a deep depression. To get it all off my mind I started small talk with Maxine. I'm sure she could tell that I was in deep thought about something in particular.

"Did you pay the car insurance this month? I got a letter in the mail this morning," I asked, lifting my glass to my lips.

"Don't I always pay it?" she said, while tugging at a braid.

"Well, last month I recall you took the bill money and ordered several outfits from Amazon. I'm sure that doesn't come to mind, now does it?"

She stopped loosening her braid and rolled her eyes in my direction. "You know what, Tim, you always got something smart to say. I worked overtime last week to make up for that money I spent, so no worries. But you wouldn't know that, since you're all in Joseph and Selina's business. By the way, Selina called earlier *again*. She said it was urgent." Her eyebrows caved in with a look of suspicion scrolled across her face.

"What did she say was wrong?"

"Oh it's probably her usual. She's sitting somewhere boo-hooing, waiting for her big brother Tim to rescue her from all of her problems. I'm sure you already saved her a few times this week. So go ahead and call her back to save her again. You continue to be Captain Save-A-Hoe for that girl," she said with sarcasm.

I slammed my glass down on the dining room table. "Why do you act like that?"

"Because she has a husband and she shouldn't be calling mine every time she has a scratch on her behind. I would appreciate it if she stopped using you twenty-four-seven and allowed her husband to help her through some of these problems. She's so troubled and needy. He probably can't help her either. Only a miracle can help that girl."

"That's why you need to pray for her, Maxine, instead of judging the situation," I pleaded. "You know what she's been through so why not embrace her and show her we love her."

She yanked her braid out once she got to the top of her head. "Everyone has been through something tragic in their life, Tim, so why is she any different?"

"That is so stereotypical and cold for you to say. You should at least try to be her friend sometimes."

"I don't have time for weak women. She ain't my cup of tea anymore. The more babies she pops out, the less of a backbone she has."

I looked back with anguish. "Really, Maxine?"

I rubbed my temple, full of worry. I wished there was a female somewhere that Selina could talk to. Too bad she wasn't fully accepted by the women at Ebenezer. She really needed a shoulder or two to cry on. My only way of helping from here on out would not be to go after Joy but to bring Selina closer to God. This situation was truly out of my hands.

CHAPTER 11- JOSEPH

I sped up when I got on I-20 West, headed towards Atlanta. It was a peaceful ride as I listened to the local jazz station. There were barely any cars on the road and a mist of dew fogged up my windows. Kenny G's rendition of Alicia Key's "I Ain't Got You" played softly.

I couldn't stop thinking about what Timothy said about Joy. Could she be one of those crazy women you see on television? Would she really try to ruin everything I had established, based on our past?

One thing I couldn't deny though, in spite of her crazy antics, she was gorgeous. She was in her fifties and looked very stunning for her age. She was a cross between Halle Berry and Janet Jackson as she carried herself like a younger woman. She dressed well, always had a made-up face, and her weave extensions were flawless. Men raved about her voluptuous shape and big eyes. Bishop was a blessed man to have someone on his arm that could still turn heads. Joy was considered to many as a complete package. Her past issues of drinking, promiscuity, and manipulating men didn't seem to harm or hurt her in the eyes of other males. Men didn't pay attention to her flaws as they fell at her feet. Bishop was lonely when his first wife left him and I guess Joy was what he thought he needed to ease the pain.

While I stepped on the gas to hit seventy miles per hour, I analyzed the entire situation.

My cell phone rang.

I pressed the Bluetooth button. "Hello?"

"Ummm, sorry to call so late, but—"

"What is it?" Joy had fear tunneling through her voice.

"It's Bishop."

"What's wrong? Stop playing games, Joy."

"No, seriously, his blood pressure dropped again and I thought you should know. The doctors say he may not make it through the night."

My fingers trembled on the steering wheel. "Are you sure?"

"Yes, I'm sure." she replied softly.

The whisper in her voice reminded me of all the late-night calls we used to have after my college football games. It was that soft and sensual tone that always had me going. Her 1-900 voice could always spin me deep into her web. I inhaled, thinking about her plump legs laying across mine when we made love. I couldn't lie, hearing her whisper vibrate through the car speakers took me back in time.

"Pray over Bishop and tell him to hold tight. I'm turning around."

"Okay," she responded, sniffling.

I disconnected, spinning the car around at the next highway intersection. I turned down the music in order to hear my own prayer that I recited slowly in my head. My thoughts became cloudy. Not only did I start to pray for Bishop to beat his illness, I also prayed for myself. Hearing Joy's voice took me down a long memory lane stroll. I was feeling warm inside as I felt my face lighting up. I mustered a smile. I thought I had my feelings under control. But apparently just hearing her voice had me floating on cloud nine. My vision was becoming blurry as I tried to remain steady on the road. My heart raced. I always assumed that there would be nothing that could come between the love of me and my wife. But the passion that remained between Joy and I just couldn't compare to any other. I was puzzled as the old feelings consumed me. The devil was busy…real busy.

CHAPTER 12–SELINA

It was close to midnight. I was feeling disoriented while having flashbacks of the murders.

A pool of blood.

A Magnum .45.

A travesty.

Two cold bodies on top of one another while laying across the living room carpet. My mother's arms were spread across the floor. Meanwhile, my father's hand remained on the gun. The crime scene constantly played like a DVD recording in the front lobe of my brain. I couldn't stop thinking about that day after finding them. I was standing there all alone as blood rushed out of their brains. My mother had the look of terror in her eyes. It was as if she died from shock before the bullet ever pierced her body. My dad lay crisscrossed over my mother's body with a permanent frown. He was face down, holding the Magnum .45 tightly. No one could hear my screams when I found them. No one cared.

The phone rang, bringing me back to life as I gasped for air thinking about the horrific scene. A soothing voice came across my headset. "Hey, babe, I'm heading back to Birmingham. There is something wrong with Bishop."

Now was not the time for him to be away helping others. I needed him more. "Right now?"

"Yes, I just turned around to go back. I will come home as soon as I finish checking everything out with him."

"Baby, I need you here," I said with garbled words.

"I know, but I have to do this, honey. It's my duty. See you in a few. Kiss the babies for me."

Your duty?

What about me?

I clicked the red button of my cell phone abruptly. I wasn't surprised at the sudden change of plans. The church and its members always seemed to take priority over our family. I could've sworn there was a scripture about supporting family first. Instead of being home with his wife and young children, he would rather run up and down the highway to rescue or fix what I considered to be unfixable people.

Baby boy had a cold, so I stayed at home in Atlanta this particular Sunday and missed out on church. Having sick children was one of the downfalls of attending a church two hours away from home. Even if Jayden felt better, driving the distance was starting to take a toll on me. I was tired and didn't seem to have much energy these days. Hauling two young children around between two car seats, double strollers, and pushing them up on each side of my hip when they both had a meltdown fest at the same time wasn't always easy.

I started to feel queasy.

I laid in my bed as the street light's vertical stream pierced into the bedroom window. Jessica and Jayden were beside me up under my arms fast asleep. Our king-size bed swallowed the three of us whole. I looked over admiring the two of them with their soft snores and peaceful looking positions. I must admit, in spite of everything that was going on, we did make some beautiful babies. Jessica looked like her father with a mocha skin tone whereas Jayden looked like me with some of my Asian features around his eyes and nose. However, they both had the Witherspoon head of hair. Thick curly locks stood on top of their heads. There was talk on having more children after Jayden. But after spending so much time alone and always worried about my husband's faithfulness or lack thereof, I didn't want to bring another child into the melodrama. Not only that, I wasn't feeling confident that Joseph would stay with me. Any woman could come along and offer him the world. My way of thinking was warped after finding those letters last year. Not only did the discovery irk my soul but it also kicked my paranoia into overdrive.

Why didn't he ever speak about having a relationship with

Joy beforehand? Was it even considered a real relationship? Or was it purely sexual? I had a hard time believing a woman of her age would take an immature young man seriously and call it a relationship. Especially in the church. I didn't see the attraction between the two of them at all. She was mouthy and uncensored while he was mysterious and private. Being an older woman with a *Stella got her groove back* kind of thirst in a church setting was not cute. Not a good match. Either way, the letters exposed it all. Joseph had no choice but to explain why the Bishop's wife wanted him so badly. I swallowed hard, thinking about it as the rage of him cheating trickled down my spine.

My friends in college warned me about men in ministry but I never believed them. They told me stories about women coming to church only to find a man and how some didn't even care about coming for God. The vultures came Sunday after Sunday for whatever they could get their hands on. *My* man seemed to be the main attraction for some of them.

I cupped my face deep into my hands, tunneling back to the very first day we met. If life could just be that simple again.

It was pouring warm droplets of rain. A gust of wind swirled around as the students rushing to breakfast ran for cover. My roommate and I skipped quickly, trudging our way to the chapel. A few basketball players were standing in front of the double doors chitchatting. When we walked in, all eyes were on us.

"Yo, Joseph. That's my sister I was telling you about," Timothy pointed.

"Hello, beautiful." I swooned, waving back, struggling to formulate audible words. They gave each other the eye while slapping hands and pumping fists using the man code for goodbye. My friend, Diamond, looked back rolling her eyes, then gave me a flabbergasted look that read, "jock alert, move with caution."

"Selina is the name. Not beautiful." We moved forward to find a seat.

Within seconds, a deep baritone voice rumbled in my ear, "Okay, Selina, but you're so beautiful."

I giggled, not knowing what else to say as his words warmed my heart. Diamond looked back, rolling her eyes again, unbothered by his masculinity. Her lips thinned as she walked ahead of us.

He seemed amused, inching behind me. His teeth glistened as he rubbed his close-cut head, throwing back a bashful grin. "Wow, Timothy didn't lie about you. The essence of your beauty captured my soul when you walked by me."

I continued to walk. "Really? How sweet."

I took my seat as he pulled a pen from his pocket. He opened the palm of my hand and said, "May I?"

I shivered at his touch. He wrote down his cell on my palm. He looked down into my eyes flashing a sensual grin and said, "I look forward to hearing from you soon, beautiful."

I gazed at the number he wrote. I could feel my skin melt like butter.

I fell deep into a trance as Diamond babbled about the half-truths of dealing with athletes. I had faith that I could win his heart and I blocked her negative rant out of my head completely. I yearned for a man like Joseph. I wanted to be loved.

At that moment, my heart pumped wildly, just thinking about how sincere he was when we first met. Then I started thinking about present day and I jumped up and started packing our bags. My disposition had gone limp as my mind twirled thinking about him being in that hospital room with Joy.

One bag for me and the other for the children.

I loaded everything in the car piece by piece. I was determined to get to Birmingham to intercede on any foul play when it came to Joy and her antics. Flushed with misery and worried about another woman wasn't getting me anywhere by remaining put. I had to get up the road fast and in a hurry.

My hands flailed with nervousness as I tried to move as fast as I could. Once all bags were loaded, I put the children into their car seats. My muscles tensed while trying to shake off self-pity. I revved up the engine to my Lexus coupe and braced the steering wheel tightly.

I started talking to myself to ensure I wouldn't chicken out on my planning. "You got this, girl. That's your man and don't you forget that," I whispered to myself. My jaw became tense as I longed for relief. I was pumped and my voice escalated. "I hope you're ready for me, heifer. He's my husband!"

CHAPTER 13-JOSEPH

After turning around, I hit the Jefferson County line in full speed. I had to get to Bishop. I felt bad about leaving my beautiful wife hanging in the wings once again. I would make it up to her when I got back to Atlanta. She was the most patient and caring woman I had ever laid eyes on and I owed her for this one. Besides, no other woman could handle all the obstacles of a busy ministry like she could. Ebenezer took up a lot of my time and she was so understanding.

I drove into Shelby Baptist Medical Center's parking lot, eager to get inside. I jumped out the car and rushed in, hoping that Bishop was still alive. When I entered his room, he was laying still and peaceful with several machines beeping around him. He was alone.

Is he really dying? Or was this Joy's way of getting me back in town? His skin looked darker than before, so maybe there was some truth to her story. His lips were cracking with a tinge of discoloration from corner to corner. The beeping of machines echoed as I monitored his body closely. His chest barely moved and I had a hard time figuring out if he was still breathing. His eyes were closed shut and his hands were folded on top of him tightly together. He looked very relaxed. Actually, he looked as if he was already dead.

"Bishop?"

He didn't move.

Joy's voice trailed behind me. "Hello there, Minister Joseph. Glad you made it back."

She walked up to the bed wearing a see-thru blouse with a halter top shell that barely covered the top of her breasts. The V-shape stopped at the tip of her cleavage line and I couldn't help but to stare down at her. I blinked away and said, "He isn't going to die, is he?"

"Yep," she answered without flinching.

"He was trying to mouth words just yesterday. What happened?"

She sighed as she reached for my hand. "It's all for the best. He's suffered way too long, don't you think?"

I pulled back, flapping my hand in the air. "Are you serious right now?" I demanded.

She stepped back with a look of irritation and folded her arms. "What else do you want me to do? He's dying, so life moves on because you're still here, right?" She inched closer with a desperate glare. "I can't stop thinking about you, Joseph." Her eyes were dreamy. Her clammy hands reached over to touch my arm.

I backed away, pointing my finger in her direction. "You're a sick individual, you know that? Your husband is on his death bed and this is how you react?"

She hissed, "Let him die. You will get the church, I will get the money and we will all be happy. Right?"

Joy looked wicked and she started to scare me. I had never seen her like this before. She had the look of a deranged psychopath killer that was ready to do more damage. Her eyes were pinkish red and her hair looked like it hadn't been combed in days.

Timothy was right…she's lost it.

"What's going on with you, Joy?"

"What do you mean?" She flickered her fingernails in my direction.

"What happened to loving only your husband?"

Her eyes were flushed as she wobbled closer, smiling. "Don't be silly. I love you and you love me, too. You just don't want to admit that. I can't help who I love. No one can."

"Why can't you accept the fact that we will never be together again?" I responded coldly.

Her eyes zoomed in as she grabbed me. "Because it's not a fact. It's something you made up in your head. I can tell how you look at me, Joseph. Everyone can see the love in your eyes when you look at me." She grabbed my hand and rubbed her breast up and down with it, while delivering a soft and sensual whisper. "Do you know how good you used to make me feel, Joseph?"

I licked my lips as sin trampled my brain cells. I snatched my hand back, secretly wishing this was a dream, so I could have my way with her and not be held accountable for my actions. Her flirtatious eyes were opening and closing as if something was wrong.

Then, it dawned on me what was going on. "Have you been drinking?"

She dropped my arm and pressed her nails into her hips as if the question cut her like a knife. "Who wants to know?" she slurred.

"Oh God, Joy." I stiffened, not pleased at the major setback of going back to alcohol for comfort.

"I know you're not surprised, are you? How else do you expect me to deal with all of this trauma?" She sniffled loudly with her eyes throwing back a look of guilt.

"Shame on you." I waved her away. Drinking was her crutch in previous years. But, we worked so hard to get her over that hump. It now became her excuse again when she needed to beam out of reality and into her own personal twilight zone.

"I worked so hard to help you beat this. Why are you

doing this to yourself?"

By the smell in the room, Hennessy was still a favorite drink of choice.

She cried, covering her face with her palms. "I know. I'm sorry. I had to drink in order to help kill him."

"It's okay…" I stopped in mid-sentence. "You what?"

She put her hands over her lips. "Oops, that's not what I meant. I meant to say all of the trouble I seem to cause is probably killing him."

I hesitated. I didn't know what to believe as her sorrowful cries were erased instantly. "Don't start blaming yourself."

"I have to, this is all my fault."

I put my hands on her shoulders and squaring her up. I looked at the top of her head. She looked a mess. It didn't help either that the alcohol she drank was seeping out of her skin. Meanwhile, her eyes were filled with lust and seduction. She hobbled closer as the pressure of my fingers seemed to soothe her and move her forward.

"Please." She begged with her hands in prayer mode. "Just hold me." She looked back at Bishop. "Can't you see he's dying? What can I do with a dying man?" she screamed. "Nothing. I can't do nothing. I won't have nothing. I need you, Joseph."

"No. Don't say that."

She moved closer, rubbing my arms up and down. "Just hold me, baby. Please. I won't ever ask again. I just need you right here and right now."

After feeling the sweat that poured down my neck, I realized old feelings were coming back in full circle. I tried to resist her touch, but her hands were like an octopus and they seemed to touch every part of my body all at once. Before I could catch myself, my hands were pressing around her waist, too.

"Please," she howled. "Make love to me."

I imagined myself taking two steps towards the door and removing her hands from my arms. But, when I looked down, my hands were still attached to her waist. Heavy breathing started as I tried to push her away. Then one of Bishop's machines started to beep. The life lines on the monitor zig-zagged as I viewed with panic.

Joy sobbed uncontrollably. "See. He doesn't need me anymore. You need me, honey."

"Don't do this to yourself, Joy," I whispered in her ear, holding her tightly.

"Oh, God. You feel so good." She put her hands over her mouth in awe. Within seconds, all the machines in the room started beeping in unison. She winced.

"Do something." I yelled. "Where is the nurse?"

She calmly reached over at the emergency cord hanging from the bed and pulled it.

"How can I help you?" the nurse asked.

"Help. Somebody help my husband. He's dying." Fear fell over her face as she came to the realization of what was really happening and then yelled, "Oh, God, he's dying!"

Footsteps could be heard all down the hallway as help came our way. My emotions jackhammered in my chest. I trembled, with my hands reaching all over Joy's back. A moment of electricity sparked between us. Our emotions were mirrored. I cried, I inhaled, and cried some more. The scent on her blouse soothed me as I now welcomed every touch. This feeling was familiar and comfortable. I released a small gasp, grabbing her closer as tears trickled down my face. With heavy breaths, we fondled one another continuously. I enjoyed feeling her warm skin against mine as she lifted her leg to put around my legs.

The painful reality was I couldn't resist her any longer. Apparently, deep down, she was missed. As her fingers trickled up and down my arms, her hands lowered and intertwined in mine, a glimmer of love shooting back and forth between us.

I remembered.

I remembered how she loved me. I remembered how I loved her. I found myself leaning in and gazing into her beautiful eyes. Our body's moved in sync together. I held her face in the palm of my hands as her lips puckered towards mine. I couldn't resist any longer. I had to taste them.

Her red lipstick was faded, but her lips still looked soft and moist. I reached down and then it happened, we kissed. As our lips locked, the hospital room door swung open. I looked up and saw tiny little feet dangling from a stroller. My children were being ushered in by their mother, my wife, Selina. I was startled and jumped back quickly, but Joy was still holding onto my chest tightly. Selina's eyes were glued to the center of the room.

"Hey, guys. I came…"

I pushed away Joy's hands as Selina gawked at our heated discretion. A howling scream of betrayal rushed out of her lips and echoed throughout the room. "What are you doing, Joseph!"

I threw up my hands in defense. "No, Selina, it's not what it looks like. I was just giving her a hug of comfort." I stepped back several feet pressing my lips together as if she just physically punched me in the mouth with her bulged eyes. The nurse ran past me to see what was going on.

"Liar!" she screamed, leaning over the stroller.

Joy responded with her hands on her hips. "Don't come up in my husband's hospital room screaming and yelling like some maniac. Can't you see my husband is dying right now?

Have some respect for your Bishop." She slumped over Bishop's body and started to chortle, "You shall live and not die!" The performance was right on time to lessen the sting of being caught. But it didn't matter, I could feel my wife's angry vibes across the room. I looked down at my babies, feeling ashamed of being caught in a lustful moment by my entire family. A strange feeling had come over me. I was convicted. I was embarrassed.

I had to make this right. I walked over and grabbed my wife. I didn't know what else to do. I hoped that holding her in front of Joy lessened her anger. She slumped down and cried in my arms.

"Why, Joseph? Why?" she asked.

"It's okay, Selina. It's okay. It wasn't intentional."

Selina leaned in closer, clutched her purse and cried even louder. As she cried, the children cried along with her. The noise level scared them and it became a disheartening scene.

"Stop all the crying," Joy mocked.

Th nurses took a few moments and pressed several buttons on each machine. We were informed that Bishop wasn't leaving us, the machines were acting up.

"Everything's fine. Apparently, his machines were acting up all day and it's just a fluke," the nurse stated.

A few more buttons were pushed and the noises faded.

We heard a mumble as we all turned towards Bishop's body.

"H…ellp meee," he whispered.

Joy lied once again. Another game to get my attention. But this time, this game might have cost me my marriage. I detected the level of Selina's rage as I continued to hold her tightly. Her purse dropped to the floor, but she still positioned one hand on the stroller while shaking. I was speechless. I looked back at Joy with disgust.

CHAPTER 14-TIMOTHY

"Good morning, Church," Joseph said.

"Good morning."

"As you know, we had a little scare with Bishop a few days ago. But thanks be to God, he is coming out of the darkness and into the marvelous light."

The congregation shouted, "Halleluiah. Thank you Jesus."

"We ask that you keep him and his family uplifted in prayer." He looked down at Joy, then back at the congregation again.

Everyone nodded, looking over at Joy with sorrowful stares. Instead of being somewhat happy of her husband's recovery, she looked displeased.

Meanwhile, Selina walked in and sat closer to the front. She wore a beautiful, tight-fighting pink suit with the shoes to match. Her natural hairstyle fit her face as her curls locked tightly on her head. She looked as if she was ready for a primetime interview with Barbara Walters, to discuss how to bounce back from baby making. Joseph smiled as she took her seat.

We sat right behind Joy on the second row. Her body shifted several times after watching the eye exchange of the two.

"Doesn't she look beautiful?" I nudged Maxine.

"About time," she hissed.

Selina didn't take her eyes off her man. Their eyes locked and then Joseph began to speak. "Church, this is the perfect time to inform you that I will be celebrating my second year of marriage with my lovely wife, Selina. We are putting together an anniversary party right here at the church in a few weeks." He stopped to catch his breath as he looked back at his wife. "Isn't she lovely? The most beautiful woman I have ever laid eyes on."

"Amen," the church reeled.

Joy coughed loudly.

Joseph continued without missing a beat. "God couldn't have given me a better mate. So, please join us for the grand celebration. We will have some good food catered for everyone to enjoy. My prayer is that Bishop will be in the house to enjoy it with us as well."

"Amen."

Joseph was handling all parts of his chaotic and fake lifestyle like a champ. He looked like an impersonator, pretending everything was good while standing up at the pulpit. "Now, if you can turn your Bibles to…"

Pages were shuffled all throughout the building, while some clicked on cell phones to pull out their Bible apps. While I searched for the scripture, a foul aroma hit my nose. I tried to remain attentive to the sermon, but the scent wasn't going to go unnoticed.

"Is that liquor? Can you smell that?" I turned to Maxine and asked.

She nodded her head as her nose followed the smell. She tried not to get directly on Joy's neck as we all knew that Joy slipped into her old habits again. She smelled like a keg of moonshine, mixed with a teaspoon of honey and Hennessy. She fanned herself as perspiration consumed the nape of her neck and arms. The more the fan moved back and forth, the easier it was for the smell to be identified. It was obvious she was out of control, without Bishop.

I heard whispers and a few giggles in the row behind us. Two old ladies started a full-fledged conversation as if they were sitting outside on their front porch, sharing the daily news.

"Is that hussy drunk in church again?"

"You know she is."

"Probably had to drink away all the guilt for making Bishop have a heart attack."

"You right about that, Sista."

They slapped a high-five, quietly leaning over with faint

giggles. It was a sad commentary. The little bit of respect folks had for Joy was washed away into the hardwood floors of the church. Maxine turned around and put one finger up to her mouth to signal to the old ladies to settle down. They continued to have a field day talking about Joy's unsettled life. She was now the laughing stock of the congregation.

I gasped at them hoping they would get back to listening to the sermon. Selina sat up tall and proud as her husband hacked loudly after every other word. She seemed much better now that people were acknowledging her as the next first lady and she dressed the part. But, that didn't stop the women of the church from doing their usual. At least they now plotted behind her back, instead of in her face like they used to. Joseph being the lead temporary preacher gave her a smidgen of power.

"I said, the miracle worker is here."

"Amen," the crowd reeled back.

"Do you hear what I say, Church? The miracle worker is already here. Now clap your hands if you love Jesus."

"Amen," I shouted in agreement.

As Joseph became louder, Joy's fake sniffles became louder, too.

"Is she sucking up that pride and pushing it to the back of her throat?" Maxine asked with sarcasm.

"Probably," I responded nonchalantly, while nodding in

agreement. Joseph came down from the pulpit to speak directly to the crowd. His gold and black preaching robe swayed with the movement of his body. He tried to get his point across to all that were listening and did it with ease.

"That woman better find Jesus before He finds her," Maxine whispered back.

I looked around at the congregation at all the beautiful women that sat attentively, hanging onto every word spat out of Joseph's mouth. At Ebenezer, he had a lot to choose from. Any man would be engulfed with all of the lovely ladies that attended faithfully just to see him. I zoomed back in on my wife by grabbing her hand. Joseph remained focused and stayed on the course of his sermon. All the women seemed to be looking at him as if he was a piece of meat. It didn't matter, Joseph was being faithful to his wife. Whatever brought on the change must have made the two of them fall deeper in love as Selina looked happy. I was misty eyed at Selina's appearance and proud that she had gotten over her slump of paranoia and depression. She looked so beautiful, it was as if she was back to her old self again. She had a glow of love that remained plastered all over her face the entire service. From a glance, she seemed somewhat whole again.

CHAPTER 15-JOY

I tried to drink away my guilt as much as I could. While spending so much time alone, I planted some crazy stuff in my head. I couldn't shake some of the feelings away even if I tried. So, I drank some more. Just when I thought Michael was going to die, he rose from the dead like Lazarus. I questioned my choices in life. I also questioned my selfish reasoning behind marrying him in the first place. I was confused. I was lonely. I was bitter. But most of all, I was drunk. I was over pretending and I stopped going to the hospital every day to see him. I felt it was a waste of time. What used to be once a day visits now turned into every other week.

After seeing the way Joseph and Selina looked at each other on Sunday, it was clear that Joseph wasn't coming back to me. At least not on his own. The plight of rejection became real as I tipped the bottle of Hennessy, thinking about it. He had love in his eyes for that little girl. I don't remember him looking at me like that. I *wanted* him to look at me like that. If I could only get him alone. Kidnapping him would be too extensive. I just wanted to tie him up, put him in my trunk and disappear.

I held my head with both hands trying to horizontally squeeze out the crazy thoughts. The lights seemed to flicker in the room. But it wasn't the lights that were going in and out. It was the bouncing of my pupils. The liquor had taken me on a journey to the land of ecstasy. I sat at the kitchen table in a daze. I would take a few sips and then tip my bottle of Hennessy into my coffee cup.

I searched my pockets for money after realizing my liquor supply was getting low. I had snatched every dollar out of Michael's account like Hurricane Andrew last week. But today, I was down to my last few dollars. The daily liquor trips were coming to an end as the money dwindled away. Michael would have me committed if he knew I ran through his account in such a short time span. As I sipped down the soothing liquid some more, a large taste of resentment followed behind it. "I'm over it, Jesus." I slumped over onto the table feeling miserable.

The sound of footsteps were heard trickling down from the staircase. When I looked up, Michael's oldest son, Robert was walking towards me. His deep voice swept down the hallway and into the kitchen. "Drinking again, huh?" he asked, while standing over me.

"Go away," I moaned, shooing him away like an irritating fly.

"I think you should be the one going away. Dad told me if

I had any problems out of you, I could have the honor of putting you out on the streets. He told me about the conversation you had with him at the hospital. Did you really talk to him about poisonous berries? He seems to think you were trying to kill him."

"I said, go away." My head pressed down on top of my hands.

"You're such a snake in the grass, Joy. But not to worry. I got a little surprise for you today, ma'am."

I slurred, "What are you talking about, Robert?"

"You will see soon enough."

I lifted my head up to look at him and asked, "You hate me, don't you?" My head bobbled, waiting for an answer.

"We all hate you, Joy. All five of us. A floozy like you should've never made it down the aisle with our father."

"Tell me how you really feel, son." I burped as Hennessy and coffee came back up into my mouth. "Don't you worry, whipper snapper. As soon as I can find some money, I'm out of here. I don't like y'all either." I squinted my eyes and stuck out my tongue. I could barely hold my head up, so I plopped on the table again making a loud thump.

Robert reached in his pocket and pulled out a wad full of money. He threw it on the table and said, "There you go, trick, now leave."

His foot thumped to the ground as if he was making a crucial statement. I guess he wanted his words to stick. Did he think I was going to scramble for a pocket full of one-dollar bills? "I've lived in this house without any problems the entire time we've been married, so get out of my face with that. Now you want to mess up what I have built with your father, huh? Not going to happen."

"You ain't built nothing but a bad reputation for yourself and our family. Looks like you got you a few boyfriends at Ebenezer since Daddy's been gone, huh?"

I snapped back with sarcasm. "So, what if I do? Your daddy can't do nothing for me, with his half-paralyzed behind."

"Slut," Robert mumbled while walking into the living room.

I perked up, wondering how anyone knew what I was doing behind closed doors. I yelled so he could hear me in the next room, "I've never been disrespected like this. Just leave me alone." I took another sip with a throaty gulp.

He yelled back. "We know you didn't love Dad and whatever you tried to put in his food didn't work."

"Why would I try to do something like that? I'm not that evil, child."

He walked back in hurriedly to get his point across. "I can't tell." He folded his arms, bucking his eyes at me.

"Sassy children with no filters. Who else was going to put up with you all anyway besides me? Huh?"

He shook his head in disgust. "Daddy must have been either real lonely or desperate to choose a whore like you to spend the rest of his life with. The entire city of Hoover knows how you get down. I heard you like women, too. You might want to stay out of the strip clubs, if you don't want your business out in the streets."

"Boy. You are a liar and the truth ain't in you." I had my eyes closed as my head bounced back and forth off the wooden finish. I was too drunk to care about what he was talking about. My brain felt like it was swimming in a large ocean full of sea creatures. I couldn't even concentrate on what the stumpy little man-child was trying to say. I guzzled down the last few sips of my concoction and tried to get up and head to the bathroom before my bladder exploded.

Then the doorbell rang.

Robert rushed forward to open it as I stood there in a pee-pee stance. There stood a Hoover sheriff with a pile of papers in his hands.

"Is Mrs. Shackleford in?"

I walked towards the door with my hand in front of my crotch. Robert looked away with a sly grin. I guess this was my surprise he warned me about. "Why yes, I'm Mrs. Shackleford."

"These are for you." He handed me the papers in his hands.

"What is it?"

"I'm here to serve you papers for eviction. You have forty-eight hours to vacate the premises."

"*Excuse me*! I'm not going anywhere, Officer, I live here."

"Sorry, ma'am, but the owner of the home—"

"I'm the owner—"

"Not according to these papers filed a few days ago. The deed doesn't have your name on it and it looks like Mr. Shackleford signed the release. If you don't leave as asked, you will be forcefully removed from the premises."

"The hell you say!" I stood up straight, hoping I didn't pee on myself already as the Hennessy flooded my intestine.

"I hope you make a peaceful decision, Mrs. Shackleford. Here you go." He handed the papers over as I reached for them slowly. I looked down at them and then down at his big feet. He was too short to have feet that big. How was he able to chase after criminals with those tree climbers? I zoomed back in, looked at the papers again and then balled them up in my hands.

I looked back at Robert as he stood behind me with a wide grimace on his face. "You evil lil bastard. After all I've done for you."

He rubbed his hands together as if he had hit the mega-million jackpot, then stood tall with an unshakable voice. "You better be glad I didn't file charges for attempted murder after you threatened my dad in that hospital. Knowing you, you probably put something in his food. Now, didn't I tell you earlier, this ain't your house?" He pointed to the door. "So, before noon today, pack your things and get out."

CHAPTER 16-JOSEPH

It was late afternoon. The sun peeked through the sky, winking at me as I went in and out of the house with furniture. Timothy stopped by to help me load and unload a few items from our Atlanta home for the children. I decided to bring more of Jessica's toys and toddler furniture to our Hoover location to ensure the children were fully occupied for the next few weeks. I had to remain in Hoover for a month, or at least until things settled down at the church. I wanted to get things right on the business side of things. So, when Bishop returned, things would continue to run smoothly. I was fortunate that I could continue my engineering job by working from my laptop as well as handle all of the church's paperwork.

Based upon Selina's scrunched facial expressions as we moved in and out, she wasn't pleased with the extended stay in Hoover. As I moved boxes back and forth, her attitude began to suck the air right out of the room.

"Why are you acting like that, Selina?"

She sat in the living room rocking chair looking distant. "I have nothing to say about the matter."

She never got over the scene in the hospital, but I was so glad she represented me well in church last Sunday. Making everyone think that all things were working together for our good with our marriage was what I expected to happen. Now that we had to stay, she had to carry that same fake smile everywhere she went without ceasing. If she was going to be considered the temporary first lady, she had to act like one.

I stood in front of her with a box full of toddler clothes and asked, "Where do you want me to put these?"

"Who cares," she screeched, throwing up her hands.

"Maybe you need to take a trip to the nail shop or something until we get this done."

"Maybe you should find a few self-help movies on Netflix on how to be a better husband."

Timothy held back his laughter as he walked past us by covering his mouth. I almost bit my tongue, trying to hold back my words. There was a lot I wanted to say. But instead, I inched closer to her seat and reached in my pocket and pulled out a one-hundred-dollar bill. "Here. Go do something to your hair, nails, feet, something."

She snatched the money out of my hands and stomped out the front door, jingling her car keys in her hand.

"I hate this life," she screamed as the door slammed behind her.

As I watched her leave out, I wondered what she could possibly be thinking. Was she that overwhelmed with church and all that came with it? After all, it was now a job for me and not a hobby. She needed to accept that.

"You playing with fire, dog," Timothy scoffed.

I was puzzled. "What did I do now? I can't win."

"What were you thinking in the hospital that night with Joy? Selina told me all about it. Man, that woman will soon end it all for you. Keep it up."

"It was an innocent mistake. Don't harp on it."

His eyebrows rose. "It was a mistake that your wife found you in your ex-lover's arms? It's a mistake that you might have to deal with for a very long time. Selina looked like she wanted to smash your head into the wall, bro."

"She will be fine."

Or will she?

I pondered at the thought. "In spite of that little mishap. I've been faithful, bro. She ain't got nothing to worry about."

"So you say," he hissed. "You know this could end if you just stay away from Joy, right? Sit down with your wife and explain what's going on inside your head. Tell her you're still trying to tame the feelings you have for the woman, so she can help you through this. I bet if you talk to her and get it out of your system she will be more than understanding. I'm sure she will appreciate your honesty, for once."

"Nah, not happening." I picked up another box and ignored his commentary.

Timothy took a breath and picked up a box as well. I stood still, clearing my throat while balancing the carboard box in my hand.

"I just wanted things to get back to being normal. I just wanted all of this to go away."

Timothy became mute and moved the boxes in silence. All I could hear was the words *I love you* echoing in my ears while walking back and forth.

I love you. I heard it again loud and clear.

I love you. I closed my eyes to embrace the voice that was ringing in my head. The sad part about the familiar voice was that it wasn't Selina's voice that chimed into my eardrums. It was Joy's.

CHAPTER 17-SELINA

I stepped into the nail shop, hoping to see a familiar face because I desperately wanted to talk to someone. Anyone that would listen would do. This isolated world I dissolved into was not normal. Being in a mega church Sunday after Sunday and not have any friends to talk to was insane. It was the only way to save face and keep the problems of our marriage hush-hush and behind closed doors. If it ever got out that Joseph was with Joy at one time or another, he would have a nervous breakdown. It had gotten to the point that I no longer attended church to seek God. I went to church to protect Joseph's image.

There was a pungent odor that was a cross between melted glue and stale corn chips. I put my shirt over my nose, trying to save myself from toxic nail fumes but it was inevitable in a shop full of acrylic and feet exposure.

I sat down in the waiting area, trying to figure out who could I call to talk to about how I was feeling. I had gotten tired of leaning on Timothy so much. But he was the only person I could think of. He was very supportive.

"You next?" a young Asian girl asked.

"Yes."

"Mani or pedi?"

"Yes, please. Both."

She led me to her station and I sat down in front of her. She grabbed my hands close to her face and said, "Oh, you tense."

I giggled at her accent. "I guess so."

"Relax. I take care of you."

Now if this young nail tech could sense my level of tension, how did I look to others? I wish I'd never allowed my college friendships to fade away. I desperately needed a girlfriend, if nothing else, just to listen to me ramble. The way it was looking, my nail tech was about to get an earful if she kept talking. She gripped my hands tightly again, dunking one hand into a mini bowl filled with hot water.

"You have husband?"

I nodded.

Her eyes gleamed. "You pretty. You black and something else right?"

"Yes. Asian."

She smiled. "Yeah, very pretty girl."

"Thank you."

"He treat you good?"

I didn't answer.

Her eyes dropped as she realized she was asking too many questions, although I was tempted to have diarrhea of the mouth and tell all.

"Just relax. We give you the complete package."

I didn't know what the complete package consisted of, but whatever it was, I was ready for it. I tried to relax and enjoy my alone time by closing my eyes and listening to the soft music that hovered about my head. I shifted my weight in the seat enjoying the moment. My phone buzzed. It was Timothy. I guess he didn't like how I left out and was worried.

TIM: YOU ALRIGHT LADY.

SELINA: YEAH JUST TIRED.

TIM: LOL STOP ALL THAT BICKERING AND MAYBE YOU WOULD HAVE SOME STRENGTH.

SELINA: SHUT UP BOY.

TIM: YOU GONNA MAKE IT. YOU SEEM SO OUT OF IT THESE DAYS. WHAT'S ON YOUR MIND?

I glanced up at the lady, giving her the side eye as she started to become rough while cleaning my cuticles on my left hand.

"Ouch."

"Oh, sorry," she said, moving the cuticle brush slower across my fingers putting her head down.

SELINA: I FEEL LIKE I'M A SINGLE PARENT.

The phone rang as I put it up to my ear with my free hand.

Timothy shouted, "What do you mean you feel like a single parent?"

"I'm doing this alone, Tim. I think I need to leave and go to an unfamiliar place and start over."

"Like where?"

"Like Boston or Syracuse. Anywhere but Hoover, Alabama, Georgia, and Ebenezer Baptist."

"It's not that bad, sis."

"Oh, yes it is. Live with me for one day and you will see it for yourself."

"Alright, so let's do our usual to get you back on track. Let's meet downtown for a cup of coffee. I've got to help you get through this one. I know where it stems from and I think I can help."

"Alright, homie. When?"

"Like in the next ten minutes."

"Dang. I'm getting my nails and feet done, dude."

"Okay, an hour?"

"Two hours."

He huffed. "Fine. You better have a smile on your face when I see you, too, lady."

"Okay… Starbucks on 9th Street?"

"That will work."

As the Asian woman looked at me with a peculiar glare, I took a deep breath, looking forward to our meeting. "Not two owa'. I will get helper to do your nail and I finish your feet sooner than that."

I shrugged my shoulders. "Okay, great."

I didn't mind how long it took. Every minute away from home counted towards mental relief. Smiling and faking for Joseph in church was one thing, but at home, I couldn't stand to look at him.

CHAPTER 18-TIMOTHY

I sat in a daze for a few minutes as I stared through Selina.

"Are you sure?"

"Yea, I got the results back yesterday."

Selina shared the news that she was pregnant again, but she also shared that Joseph gave her a venereal disease.

"So, are you going to say something?"

"Not really."

"Sis, you have to. He needs to know that he's been caught red-handed. Who do you think it came from?"

She gave me the stupid face. "Really, Tim. You know dog on well who he slept with."

"He hadn't said a word to me about another woman. I'm just a little shocked right now."

"Don't be." She put her hand up like a stop sign.

"I'd rather it be anyone but Joy. That woman is going to hurt someone if she can't have him all to herself one day."

"You have so much faith in your brother, don't you? You really believe he can just sit around all those beautiful women and keep his pants up? Do you really believe that in a church with two services and over one thousand members that attend between the two that he is faithful? Tsk tsk."

"I get it, sis. I do. But, you can't keep living in silence or in fear. When things happen, you need to talk about it. Get it out and let him know how you feel. He is guilty as well because he won't tell you the truth. But, you can't keep playing this happy couple role when you know it's all wrong."

"I hear you." She propped her elbow on the table with a frown.

"So now I understand why you were so upset this morning. It wasn't because he was asking you to remain in Hoover. It was because of all of this."

"Yep."

"How far along are you?"

"Four months."

"How do you feel?"

"I feel fine. They gave me antibiotics to take, but eventually he will have to take some, too, in order to get rid of it."

I leaned back. "Unbelievable."

"Yeah, I wouldn't make this up." She gave a long sigh as tears streamed down her face. "Why would God do this to me? Why would God allow me to be with a man who doesn't love me?"

"He loves you, sis. He just doesn't know how to keep you, that's all. It's gonna be okay."

I rubbed her forearm, trying to comfort her as much as possible. The truth is, I was just as shocked as she was. It was clear that Joseph had lost his ever-loving mind.

CHAPTER 19-JOY

Michael had months of therapy ahead of him. I needed him to come home, so I could plead to re-enter the house without any friction from his kids. I knew since I hadn't visited him in the hospital for a while that moving back without him wasn't an option. Meanwhile, I was moving from pillar to post, trying to make it after being put out of our home. I immediately moved out as asked and never looked back. Motel 6 was my off and-on-residence, depending on how much cash I had on hand. Otherwise, the back seat of my car became my safe haven. The hotel was across the street from a boarded-up Church's Chicken restaurant and the neighborhood wasn't at all safe. It was a dingy, tiny space with mold all around the windows. The darkened throw rugs in the middle of the floor carried a stifling odor. I couldn't help but to gaze around with disgust each time I entered what was now my home.

This is not how I planned to live my life.

But, in spite of my living situation, being with Joseph again was magical. I knew he loved me and I knew that one day I was going to get the chance to lay in his arms again. It happened so fast and considering I was a little tipsy that night, I tried to remember it all.

"Joy, why are you here?"

"I was circling around the neighborhood and I didn't see your wife's car. Is she home?"

"So, you're following me around now?"

"Don't be so surprised, honey. When I called you last night, I meant what I said. I was going to see you today. Is there a problem?" He looked down my shirt, mesmerized.

"No problem at all."

I guided his hand and then he guided mine. I had a bag full of gin and juice and I was ready to celebrate our reunion. Within seconds, he whispered softly, *"Come on in. Selina is at the Atlanta location at a birthday party with the kids."*

"Party time then." I swiped his chin with my fingernail.

He walked to the kitchen to get a glass as I made my drink mixture. He couldn't take his eyes off me.

"So, what made you give in finally?"

"The night at the hospital."

I gave a devilish grin. *"Come here."*

He kissed me passionately and I kissed, sipped, and kissed again. He laid me down on the floor of his living room and made love to me. As the portrait of his family sat on the bookshelf across from us, I was not fazed. I was enjoying all that he was willing to give. I had finally gotten my man *back.*

Such sweet memories. I was ready to be with him once again.

CHAPTER 20-JOSEPH

What a way to wake a brother up. I ruffled the covers, staring into her eyes.

"Pregnant? Again?"

"That's what happens when people have sex without a form a birth control you know."

"But, Selina, we just started getting back to normal after Jayden."

"What is normal to you? Does that consist of me making you look good in front of your congregation?"

"Selina, don't start, babe. We've been getting along so well these days."

"In the eyes of who?" She rolled over and slapped her hand on my chest.

Child number three... I wasn't ready. Now I wished she would get her tubes tied. This was way too much for me. All the bottle fixing and baby food mixing cereal was going to start all over again. It was getting really old.

"Our children are too close together in age, Selina. This is difficult."

"Get a nanny then. You got the money. You want to lay me on my back, but not be accountable when the babies arrive. Shame on you."

I doubled back. "What's up with your mouth? You've never talked to me this way."

"Get pregnant back to back like me and see what your mouth would do."

Was she trying to prove something by having all these babies? A doggone baby making machine times two. I was already trying to fight back the lust demons inside of me for wanting Joy again and now this? I didn't have time for a side chick and I didn't have time for more babies either.

Hiring a nanny was definitely next on my to-do list.

I rolled over to hold her tightly in my arms while brainstorming my next sermon. "Shhh, let's just be quiet for a few minutes. Let's meditate on how we will enjoy our next child." I rubbed her belly as we lay there stiff. Before I knew it, sunlight had broken through the window and it was time for church. "I love you, Selina. Do you still love me?"

She didn't flinch.

Instead, she turned around to look me in my eyes with a dead pan stare. Her voice was raspy as if she had eaten a bag of cotton. "Do I have a choice?"

I smiled back. "You always have a choice, honey. No one

is holding you hostage."

"Whatever. If that's the case as soon as I deliver I'm moving up north." She shuddered.

"What? You just need some sugar that's all. Come over here so I can give you a kiss. You talking crazy." I kissed her lips gently, but she didn't move. I was waiting for a smile to flicker across her mouth, but she was stiff with a stone face.

"Are you okay? What's going on?"

Her eyes blinked. "Do you miss her?"

"Miss who?"

"Joy." She sighed.

"Here we go again." I was hoping to get a last-minute invitation of morning lovin', but instead we were back to square one with her paranoid thoughts.

"Let it go, Selina."

"It's the way you look at her sometimes in church. You look at her as if you still care about her."

"Stop it, Selina. I care about everyone. You're seeing what you want to see and not what is really there."

She looked at me and said, "Don't talk to me like I'm crazy. I know what I see."

"Selina, we have two beautiful children, a lavish home in two locations, and a good life together. Why do we need to keep bringing up the past? Why are you so fixated on what I did before your time? I wouldn't have gotten married to you if I wasn't ready to be fully committed to only you."

She looked over and said with a calm tone, "That sounds so interesting, love. Let me show you something." She reached for her purse on the nightstand and pulled out a stack of papers.

"Hold on, let me use the bathroom first. What is it the baby's heart beat or something?" I jumped out of bed and slid my bedroom slippers on my feet, speed-walking towards the bathroom.

"Nope."

I couldn't think of anything else she could've had going on that I needed to see, knowing we had to get ready for church.

"What is it then, honey?" I flushed the toilet, washed my hands and then walked back over to the bed.

She raised up and said, "Read this, darling."

I didn't know what to make of her facial expression as she seemed cold and distant. Was she having another flashback of her parents? Did some form of inheritance show up from their death?

I picked up the papers and pulled them close to my face. The word *Gonorrhea* was in big bold letters.

"What is this about? You've been sleeping with someone?" I asked, baffled.

"Are you serious right now, Joseph?" She pushed the

covers off and stood up straight with her hands on her hips. She took out a bottle of pills, walked over and shook them in my face.

"Whoever you are cheating with, you might want them to know that they are walking around spreading their nasty germs onto my husband's penis and infecting our unborn child. Get it together, Joseph, or else I will embarrass the hell out of you this morning. Do you hear me!"

As the pills continued to rattle, I stood with my mouth open. One night of passion with Joy had now turned into a clinic visit with a side of antibiotics.

"I... I..."

"Don't you open your mouth and say one word you lying, cheating—"

I grabbed her before she could finish. I was so ashamed. I should've known better.

"I need help, Selina. I need help," I cried.

"You need help, alright."

"Joy just has some type of power over me and I haven't been able to shake it. I'm so sorry I did this to you. I'm so sorry." I held her close and cried on her shoulder. What have I done? A perfect family, a perfect wife, a perfect marriage was now slipping away. Why did I allow this?

She lifted her head back to speak. "Joseph, God will

forgive you, but you need to figure out how to remain faithful or else I'm gone. Children and all. You seem to take my kindness for weakness. I'm stronger than you know. If I can live through finding my parents dead in their home, I can live through a lying husband who cheats on me. I advise you to get it together or else it's over."

She stepped back, walked to the bathroom and shut the door. How was I going to be able to preach this morning after all of this? I messed up. I messed up bad. My problems were now bigger than keeping Ebenezer intact. I didn't have a plan of recovery, so I kneeled down in front of the bed, asking God to forgive me for my sins.

CHAPTER 21-JOY

Ebenezer was no longer a Sunday ritual for me. A bottle of whiskey or Hennessy was now my altar and sex was my pulpit. It wasn't like anyone would miss me anyway. The members probably didn't think twice, once I stopped going to church. I gave up on it all because I got what I wanted the most, Joseph.

I leaned against the smeared window for several minutes consuming the half-filled bottle of brown liquor that remained wrapped in the paper bag it came with. I wanted to drink as much liquor as possible to wash away everything around me. Within seconds, the entire bottle was demolished. I wiped my lips clean and as soon as I placed it back on the window pane, I heard a knock at the door.

I looked through the window. "Joseph?" I questioned through the door.

"Yes. Open up, Joy."

I opened the door as he rushed in and grabbed me by my neck.

"Joseph?" I gagged.

"You got the nerve to burn me, huh? You filthy hoe. This

is what you give me after all these years of waiting to have me again. I oughtta…" His hand reared back as I screamed.

"Joseph, no. What are you talking about?"

"My wife is pregnant with a venereal disease that *you* gave me. Not only did you put me at risk, you have put my unborn child at risk, too."

"Nonsense." I coughed.

"Seriously? Seriously?" He pushed me up against the wall. Above my head was a picture of a tree that was part of the hotel décor. It crashed to the floor as glass shattered everywhere.

"You better be lucky I am who God says I am, or else I would kill you for ruining my life."

I wrestled with his hand and broke free from his hold. "How dare you come in here and put your hands on me? Who the hell do you think you are?"

"I am the best man you've ever loved, that's who I am. You stay away from me, Joy. Stay away from my family. Stay away from the church. Don't you ever let me see you in the streets." He grit his teeth patting his hands onto his thighs.

I put my hands on my hips. "I'm not scared of you, Joseph." He charged again, pushing me on the bed with his hands tightly around my neck as his veins popped out of his head. "I swear to God, if any of this gets out, I will make sure the folks of

Hoover run you out of here. You hear me. You won't be able to go to the corner store alone. I promise you that."

"Please. Please stop. I can't breathe. Stop, Joseph, you're hurting me. Stop."

His eyes were bloodshot red as sweat dripped from his nose onto my face. He realized he was a few seconds away from killing me, so he got up and brushed himself off. He walked towards the door and stopped. "Remember what I said, Joy. I'm not playin'."

I sat up in the bed full of fear.

What just happened?

All the time it took to get him back and now he was gone out of my life for good, just like that? The last man I slept with was married. How in the world did I get some form of disease? I plopped my head down on the bed. My buzz was completely gone as skin peeled from my neck. I couldn't believe this. After all I've done for that nigga and this is how he treats me? I had to catch my breath and shake it all off. Little did Joseph know, he hadn't seen the last of me yet.

CHAPTER 22-SELINA

Five months later...

Our new baby, Josiah, had arrived and he was keeping me on my toes. He had colic his first few weeks of arrival and cried day and night. I was so frantic about having all of these daily duties. Motherhood wasn't very kind to me this time around as I ached all over my body. The only positive in my life after giving birth was having my husband home more often. After being caught, he settled down tremendously. The cocky and talkative man I used to know was now at my beck and call whenever I needed him. I enjoyed the newfound attention and I was going to use it to my advantage.

I rose up from the couch and put on my shoes and jacket. He looked at me funny as he fed Josiah his bottle. The other two were upstairs with the nanny. I was finally getting relief.

"Where you going?" he asked.

"I need some fresh air. I'm going to meet Tim at the coffee shop."

"Okay. Can you bring me back a piece of lemon pound cake?"

I kept walking without giving an answer. I was still vexed and I had a hard time moving forward from this last episode. Each time we went through something, anger chipped away at my heart. I started to love him less and didn't feel the same way as before. The truth is, now that I had him where I wanted him, I didn't want him anymore. It didn't seem fair to me that he could do so many hurtful things and yet I still had to love him. Society wanted me to stand tall and be the strong, God-fearing wife in spite of. But, who cares about what society thinks?

An hour later, I walked in the rain, headed towards Starbucks to meet Timothy. Although I had an umbrella in my hand, I allowed the rain to coat my face, hoping each rain drop would permeate my soul and flush away all of my worries. I stroked my cheeks with my free hand, moving dreamily to the front door of the building.

Timothy walked in Starbucks hurriedly, trying to escape the rain. He wore a bashful smile. I looked up as he stood in front of me. "Hey, beautiful."

He was dressed for work in his police officer's uniform. I repositioned myself, trying to hide my bitter smirk. Our bodies touched for a warm embrace as my emotions overtook my voice. I could barely mumble a word as I cried on his shoulder.

"Sis?" His deep voice lingered. "Are you okay?"

I shrugged my shoulders with no response. He looked me up and down escorting me to my seat. "What can I do for my little sis today?"

I had to blink away my tears. "I don't know where to begin, Timothy."

"Let's start with, hello." He chuckled. "All this crying and carrying on. You know you can't act like this when I'm on my way to work."

I flashed a grin. "Yes, I know when you are carrying that gun on your hip, you feel empowered to hurt someone for me."

We laughed in unison as I wiped my tears away.

"Being married is stressful."

"But is it really all about the marriage, sis?" he whispered as he leaned in.

"I honestly don't know at this point."

"You're too cute to be looking like life is going to end for you today. Smile, lady." He chuckled. "I just want to see you happy, sis. I remember that look from years ago after your parents died. But those babies need you and they need you healed. I know you don't believe this is post-partum that you're dealing with, but to be honest, you carry every sign of it. You can't just keep having babies back to back and think you're not going to feel bad at times. It's natural. Along with Joseph's escapades, I'm sure it all crashed down at once."

"I guess you're right." I looked away.

He shook his head back and forth. "I know, sis. I know. Now that he is helping, accept it and let your body get some rest. You might want to stop procreating until you get completely healed emotionally and physically." He ogled over at my frowning face. "By the way, I know why you keep getting pregnant and it's not due to missing birth control either."

Timothy knew me well. I thought the more children I pushed out for my husband, the more he would love me and give me the attention I longed for. I reluctantly sat up straight and wiped my face with my hands, changing the subject. "How's Maxine?"

He rolled his eyes. "Still the same ole Maxine. I haven't gotten a home cooked meal in over a year." He laughed loudly.

"Well, at least you are faithful to her." I looked down.

"Sis, don't beat yourself up about all of this. You have to take the good with the bad. You will get through it and I do believe the best is yet to come."

"So you say."

"You will, sis, and if this helps any… Joseph isn't cheating on you anymore. He's been talking to me on a regular about his situation. The struggle of being attached to that woman is over. I don't think you will have to worry in the future. He is really after God's own heart now."

He patted my hand and plopped it in the center of the table. Timothy didn't have a problem with laying everything out in front of me. He allowed me to see it for what it was. The question of being faithful didn't circulate in my head anymore. At this point, I didn't care who he laid down with. I had emotionally checked out completely.

"You think you know me so well, don't you?"

"Pretty much," he smirked. "No marriage is perfect, but I know that Joseph tries really hard, to make sure you have all that you need. He wants you happy. I want to see you happy, too, sis."

"Hey, let me take you for a ride." Timothy suggested.

"Like where?"

"It's a surprise."

"I have to take the kids to their grandparents' in a few hours."

"No worries, it won't take long."

We walked out as the metal on his uniform clanked with every step. He walked me to his black BMW that was parked in front of the building. He opened my door as I slid across the leather seats, pushing the bottom of my dress to the side. He cracked a few jokes and revved up the engine. I would come back later to get my vehicle and was anxious to see this so-called surprise.

"So, are you going to give me any details as to where we're going?"

He looked over and then back at the road. "It's just one of my favorite places. I think you will like it. I go there sometimes to get my head straight when Maxine is giving me hell. The scenery is breathtaking and it's rarely anyone there. It's probably the perfect place for you to relax when you need time alone."

"How did you find it?"

"I stumbled across it a few years ago. I never told anyone about it. It's my special getaway spot."

I pondered. "I see."

He flashed a sly grin and said, "Eventually, you will have to allow God to do the work. You can't rely on me for the rest of your life. Your faith should supersede it all at this point. So I believe this place will help you get to where you need to be spiritually and emotionally. It has an anointed kind of feel to it."

I was so dependent on Timothy that I never even fathomed going to God first. I looked straight ahead, feeling as if my best friend was dumping me.

Silence filled the car for the rest of the ride. We arrived at his spot a few minutes later. He came around the car to open my door. He grabbed my hand gently as his soft palm led the way. I slid out of the front seat and looked around at the remarkable view. It was breathtaking, just as he described it. It was a large, brown-watered river with a mini restaurant in front of it. Beautiful swans walked side by side as they bobbed their heads looking for food. There wasn't too many people around and it was very quiet. A cool breeze hit us as I closed my eyes enjoying it.

When I opened them, I asked, "How in the world did you find this? I thought we would never get down that long winding street."

"Didn't I tell you it was beautiful?"

Christmas tree lights hung above the tables while attached to the large columns that surrounded the entire property. It gave a small Italian restaurant feel with an ambiance of peace and serenity. It was truly a perfect hideaway to soothe my mind. I looked back at the water as the wind ruffled its waves and then at him.

"So, I guess this is the moment you tell me that I can't keep calling you with my problems, huh?"

He pulled me closer to the edge of the water. "Not at all. But, it is the moment that I am telling you to come here and talk to God about it. You remember when we were kids and we had that pond in our neighborhood?"

"Next to the playground?"

"Yes, that's the one. You remember that day when we went to play hide and go seek with some of the other kids and it took us hours to find you?"

I scratched my head trying to remember. "No, I don't recall."

"You had to be around eight or nine back then. Everyone was so worried that you had been kidnapped or something. We eventually found you sitting on the edge of that pond with your legs crossed, throwing rocks into the water. You were so happy and free and you sang 'You Are My Sunshine' for hours. You don't remember that?"

I scratched my forehead again not having a clue on what he was talking about. "No, sorry, I don't remember not one bit."

"Well, after that day we realized that you really loved to play in water. It seemed to calm you and you would sit there for hours not saying one word."

"Really?"

"Yep. My photographic memory can be worth something at times." He clasped his hands together. "So, I thought about your past experience with water and said to myself, maybe if I took her to my hideaway, she could sit on the bank. I saw you in the spirit enjoying it and throwing rocks, just as you did when we were kids."

I paused for several minutes. After losing my parents, I had arrested development and couldn't really remember anything about my childhood. "Thank you for bringing me here. I guess you can stop worrying about me now, huh?" I chuckled. "I will come here and give it all to God as you suggested."

He gave a wide smile. "That was my goal, sis. Seek God in this situation and every situation thereafter. I know it looks like He isn't working on your behalf, but He is. You will be my little sister no matter what, so don't take this personal. I am just showing you another way to vent. But, only God can turn this thing around for you, I just don't have that type of power."

I gazed back at the water then back at him, clearing my throat. "You are my sunshine…" As I tried to sing the song as he remembered, I was flooded with several memories. He put his arm around my shoulder and drew me close to his side.

"It's alright, sis. Let it all out."

I broke down right in front of the water. "It hurts."

"I know. But, God hasn't failed you yet. Let's give our special place a name, shall we?" He reared his head back for confirmation.

"A name?" I scratched my chin.

"Sure, why not," he said with a pleasant tone. "Let's call it, The Weeping River."

I took a deep breath, inhaling all of the fresh air around me. "That sounds depressing."

"Well, isn't this the place where you will weep for a night and allow joy to come in the morning?"

"You are too funny."

He put out his palm for a handshake. "Let's make a pledge."

I chuckled. "What? A pledge about what? Oh you are really taking it back to our childhood, huh? I haven't made a pledge with you in ages."

He stuck his pinky out, waiting for my pinky to attach to his. "Promise that you will not give up on God, Selina."

"What?"

"You heard me, sis. I can tell you've given up on not just your husband but God as well. The Bible says, 'for God so loved the world that he gave his only begotten son, that whosoever believeth in him shall not perish, but have everlasting life.' I need you to believe Selina that God is going to make a way out of no way. I need you to trust with all your heart and promise me that you will never give up. Your future is bright and God is not going to put more on you then you can bear."

I looked down at his finger and latched on. I took a deep breath and said, "Okay." He was right. I had given up on God.

I had given up on myself and had even contemplated taking my own life. I looked up at him and responded, "I promise."

"Release it all and leave it right here. Throw all your cares into this water. The old folks used to call it the sea of forgetfulness. Let this be your sea of forgetfulness."

I wailed out a loud cry and felt free to do so. As the moisture from the water brushed against my face, freeing me from my troubles, I was thankful for Tim. I was thankful for life. I was even thankful for a tinge of strength…the little bit I had left.

CHAPTER 23-SELINA

The Weeping River did eventually become my favorite place. Somedays, it was therapeutic for me. While other days, I felt like jumping in it. Timothy was right. Casting all of my problems into the water did feel good when I allowed it. If I allowed it. I had my staring into space days, balling up my fist days, crying days, and lifting up my hands and praising God days.

Each time, I went alone. I learned to enjoy the solitude. I stopped calling Timothy every time I had a pain or ache about something. I allowed God to do all of the work. As I sat writing in my journal, my cell phone rang.

"How's it going, sis?"

"I'm getting there."

"I haven't heard from you lately. I don't know how to take your silence."

"I've taken your advice. Not all of it but most of it. I've been spending a lot of time at The Weeping River."

"Something going on I need to know about?"

"Nothing really..." I paused. I did have things that I

wanted to share but I didn't want to bother him.

"Did Joseph get that nanny you asked for?"

"Yea, she started when we brought Josiah home from the hospital."

"Good. Didn't I tell you? He is working hard to give you everything you need," he said sarcastically.

We both chuckled.

"Rest assured, things are looking brighter."

"Good. I have to get to work. Keep that head up, sis."

"I will."

We disconnected the call as I sat still looking at the water. "Lord, give me happy thoughts." I wasn't completely healed but I was striving to get there. I was making progress in understanding my patterns of sadness and the triggers behind it. I smiled sardonically at the swans that walked around on the restaurant patio. I clutched my chest, unleashing more pain. My new thought process was as fresh as the morning rain that trickled into the water. Only God could give me what I needed. It wasn't my husband. It wasn't a house full of children. It wasn't even the medication I started taking to soothe post-partum. It was the Father, Son, and the Holy Spirit. I was feeling revived and although sometimes my mind wandered, I wasn't ready to give up on *me*. I wanted to live a happy life. I pulled up my Bible app on my cell phone and started reading scriptures about moving mountains and getting out of low valleys. My shiny face reflected off the screen of the cell phone. For once I saw beauty and not the ugly duckling I always considered myself to be. At that moment, I felt empowered to conquer the world. I was making progress and I wanted this feeling to last forever.

CHAPTER 24-JOSEPH

"Leaving?" She gawked.

I blew my breath, not understanding where the change in heart came from. One-minute, Selina wanted to rush back to Atlanta and now all of a sudden, she wanted to remain in Hoover. But, that wasn't possible with Joy needing a place to stay. Although I vowed to not be intimate with her, I still couldn't let her go astray and remain homeless. I paid for a few nights at the Marriott downtown until I could get Selina and the children out of the Hoover location. I planned to let her stay in our home until she could do better. I knew if I tried to explain to Selina that Joy was homeless, she wouldn't have it nor would she understand why I was doing it.

"Wait, let me get this straight. So now you don't want to go back to Atlanta?"

"No. I've gotten used to Hoover and the help given when dealing with our children. Your parents and the nanny have been wonderful to the kids. I figured why not let them continue with the same routines?"

"What the...there is nothing in Hoover but a mall and a

few antique shops. You can't be serious. You've always said you would never live here permanently. Plus, I need to get back to Atlanta to catch up on a few things."

She rubbed her hands together. "Yes, I'm very serious. Now is not the time to be moving back. I'm tired of this back and forth."

"But, you said yourself a few months ago that you had gotten tired of Ebenezer and all the baggage it carried. I was even going to try to find us a secondary church to fellowship with. Now suddenly, you have a change of heart?" I gave a stern look trying to read her cynical mind. Selina displayed bizarre behaviors lately and not wanting to move back to Atlanta confirmed that she'd been sipping Hoover's tap water. I found myself gritting my teeth and tried to maintain a straight face. I hadn't been mad at Selina in a long time but today she had pushed down on all of my patience buttons. Joy needed the space until Bishop returned. How would it look if I allowed her to remain homeless?

Her eyes widened. "Maybe I don't know what I want right now. Give me a day or two to think about it."

"I really wish you'd make up your mind soon."

"What's the big rush?"

I looked away as she grabbed my hand and kissed it. "Time is of the essence, babe. Let's sleep on it a few more nights, okay?""

I was finally being the husband that she needed me to be. But this time Joy needed me more. I couldn't believe after all of the late-night arguments of moving back and forth that my wife wanted to remain in Hoover, Alabama. I was trying to do something good for both of them. When it's all said and done, Joy Shackleford was still my responsibility. Bishop would expect me to take care of his wife, being that I was his assistant. It was my duty to take care of his family while he was down and I'm pretty sure he wouldn't have wanted it any other way.

CHAPTER 25-JOY

Where am I?

When I rolled over on my back, I felt something bumping against my knee. I turned around to discover it was an unknown body snuggled up beside me. I could feel a hairy leg rub up against me. It was obvious it was a man's leg but where did he come from? Whoever he was, he was snoring louder than a pig snorkeling in a pig pen and smelled like a bathtub full of Hennessy. He rolled over grabbing me close, opening his eyes, and smiling hard.

"Good morning, First Lady. What a night, right?"

I gasped. "What?"

"You don't remember?"

"How did you get in my bed?"

He lifted his head up. "You're joking right? You were all over me in the car last night. So, we found a bar and grabbed a few drinks. You practically undressed me on the dance floor. Then you offered a night cap." He rubbed my breast. "Who could say no to all of this beauty?"

I squinted my eyes trying to remember. The more I looked

at him the more I sat in disbelief. He flirted with his eyes as I laid there confused.

Dang, what's his name?

"You ought to be ashamed of yourself taking advantage of me like this." I pulled the covers off of me and moved to the edge of the bed.

He huffed. "Oh you need to stop, woman. If anything, I was the one that was being taken advantage of."

I gasped, wanting to hide under the bed in shame. "Say what?"

Name please…

"Oh, now you have selective memory, huh? You don't remember saying that to me last night?"

I didn't mumble a word as he sat up and grabbed me, pulling me closer to him. Whoever he was, he was making my skin crawl.

"It's not like that. I was drunk."

I need to stop all this drinking ASAP.

He edged closer. "Yeah, you were smashed. You was doing it up last night."

"Huh?"

"You don't remember? Karaoke? Dancing on the bar table? Several games of pool?"

"I'm sorry. I don't remember anything that you're speaking

of." I held my hands over my face.

"As long as you're sober enough to remember me now. Maybe when you get yourself together, later on, we can try this again…the sober way. I enjoyed you last night." He rubbed my leg gently.

It felt as if spiders were crawling down my back when he said that. "You gotta go."

He looked over surprised. "So soon? We're just getting started, baby."

I rubbed my head, pushing my hair back and feeling insulted. He wasn't even cute. He had a large nose with a receding hairline that required a close haircut. With his pot belly bumping me in the back, I was appalled. I usually didn't do his type. I must have been really desperate last night.

"You okay?" He looked over with concern.

"Yes. I'll be fine. I need you to leave."

"Will I see you again soon?"

I put my clothes on and looked back with shock. How dare he ask me that. "I doubt it."

He put on his clothes with a look of sheer disappointment.

What an ugly man.

I know that isn't his toes curled up like that.

And that receding hairline is talking to me right now.

I walked him to the door and rushed out of the hotel.

Oh what a night.

"By the way…what's your name again?"

He gasped. "Now, I'm really hurt you don't know my name, Ms. Joy. I used to go to Ebenezer years ago and I was a faithful member."

"And."

"Scott is the name." He stood outside the doorway facing me.

I didn't flinch. "Have a nice life, Scott." I slammed the door in his face and crawled back into bed. Joseph would lose it if he knew I was sleeping with strange men in the hotel room he paid for. I was lost for words as I stroked my neck, wondering what in the heck just happened.

CHAPTER 26-SELINA

I reminisced on the words Joseph said to me that day in his parents' living room when he proposed.

"I will never do you wrong and I will always protect you."

I also thought about the charge Pastor Shackleford gave us on our wedding day. He told us to love one another through the good and the bad. He charged us to rise above any adversity and never stop believing in the power of love. I sat feeling lackadaisical. I just wished I could erase the bad and start all over again from day one.

I really tried hard to have that radical faith church folks talked about. But, it hadn't arrived yet. I believed God was fixing it, but it just wasn't happening fast enough. I was on a road to redemption, but instead I was walking down a one-way street of disbelief.

I played with a squeezy ball I left on my nightstand, trying to make sense of my life. I didn't look at Joseph the same. I felt that   everything I ever loved was taken or tarnished. My parents, my marriage, my relationships… I felt like I was losing my mind.

"Hey, babe." Joseph bent down and kissed my hand.

I was reading Michelle Obama's new memoir, hoping to get some form of empowerment.

"We need to talk." I looked him dead in his eyes, not acknowledging his desire to embrace me. I felt my eyes drooping as he stared through me, waiting for me to speak my peace.

"Okay, what's up, beautiful? Did you get a good night's rest?"

"Yeah, Jayden finally went to sleep around four a.m. but I'm still exhausted."

"I can tell." He moved in closer, giving a gentle touch across my face.

"Joseph, there is something I must confess."

He sighed. "Don't tell me you found more letters or something to that nature? I haven't done anything wrong, I promise."

Hit dogs always howl.

"No, actually for once, that isn't on my mind."

"Oh." His eyebrows caved in as he flashed a look of surprise.

"I have another setback."

"Set back?"

"Yes. I don't want this anymore."

"Want what?" His mouth dropped wide open.

"This thing we call marriage. I'm having a very hard time forgiving you. I just can't get over what you did to me."

"Babe, we have to move past this. Now, I am willing to do whatever I need to do to keep you. What do you want? A trip? Counseling? A new car? Just tell me and I will make it happen."

His face lit up like a Christmas tree as he grabbed me and lifted me off the floor. "*I love you*, lady. Don't do this."

I gave a half grin. "Yeah."

"What does that mean?"

"Is it that you want to keep me because you love me, or is it you want to keep me to save your reputation with the church?"

"What do you mean?" His face scrunched in disbelief.

"I can't do this anymore." I put my hands over my face as he grabbed me closer.

"Ah, baby. Life will be so different when Bishop gets back into his role. Trust me. We are almost to the finish line."

"I can't do this, Joseph."

He put his hand under my chin and lifted my head up. "Let today be a new day, babe, and let's forget about all of my mistakes of the past, please."

I didn't feel a sense of comfort and he needed to leave *ASAP*.

"You need to leave."

"And go where?"

"Go back to Atlanta for a while. I can't do this."

"But, Selina—"

"Don't *Selina* me. I need to have some space. I need to be away from you for a while."

He put his head down and reached to kiss my hand again.

"If that's what you want, babe, I will be gone by tomorrow."

He stood up tall and walked out of the room. I didn't know if it was the right thing to do. I just needed some time to be away from him. It was time to heal.

CHAPTER 27-JOSEPH

"Lord, help us." I screamed.

I hit the brakes, not noticing the light had turned red. The last thing I needed to do was leave my family. Joy was constantly in my ear saying sweet nothings and I didn't need that type of temptation to come around twice. Common sense should have told me to stay away from that trifling woman. But, for some reason, I felt indebted to her.

Why?

I guess the soul ties were stronger than I thought. But I had to continue to be a faithful husband and trying to take care of the Bishop's wife wasn't the answer. I looked over at her as she sat beside me, grinning hard. "What does the Lord need to help us with today, honey? Are you taking me to get something to eat?"

Yep, I fell for it again. Driving Ms. Joy as if I was a slave that could not get unchained from my master.

"Joy, my wife has put me out. I can't keep helping you like this. You need to go to that rehab center and plead with your husband to give you some money. You have ruined my life."

She laughed out loud. "*Ruined* your life? Nah, you ruined mine. If you would've married me instead of that little girl, we would be happy right now." She rubbed my arm.

I drew back. "Stop it, Joy."

"Touchy this morning, aren't you?" Her fingernails flailed.

"Listen, forget everything I said about helping you okay? I won't be moving you into the Hoover home because my family is still there and I need to stay away from you from here on out."

"You are talking crazy this morning. Now get me something to eat and stop all this nonsense."

I could hear the Lord speak to me clearly about my situation. Suddenly, I stopped the car in the middle of traffic and said, "Get out."

"Say what?" Her eyes beamed into my skin.

I reached over and opened the passenger door. "I said, get out. You've done enough damage. I want my family. I'm done dealing with you."

"How am I going to get back to the hotel?"

"Not my problem."

"Really, Joseph?" She hit my arm. "Don't do this. I need you now more than ever."

"You don't need me. You need Jesus. Now get out."
Cars behind us were beeping their horns as I sat in an

intersection of traffic.

She crossed her arms. "I'm not going anywhere."

"Oh yeah?" I jumped out the car and walked around to the passenger side. I jerked the door and grabbed her by the arm. I pulled her away from the car, slammed the door shut, and walked back to the other side. "Find another sucker. I'm done."

I peeled off, leaving her standing in the middle of the road next to the yellow line. I could hear her screaming faintly as the car sailed down the road. "Joseph Witherspoon, come back here! Come back here, you hear me!"

I took a deep breath. I wasn't going to lose my family for a piece of booty. It was time to be real with myself.

Was I helping because I wanted another sexual encounter?

Did I really care about her well-being as I tried to make myself believe? Either way, it was time to end the shenanigans and come up with a plan on how to get my wife back. I might have been delayed on acting like a husband, but my future happiness with my wife was not going to be denied.

CHAPTER 28-JOSEPH

It's been said that church folks are supposed to be focused solely on God and allergic to drama. Not so at Ebenezer Baptist Church. It was a late Wednesday afternoon. I sat in the usher's meeting room, calculating expenditures from our last brethren outing. Timothy entered into the office with unconceivable news.

"Eh hmm…can I come in?" He rubbed his bony, dark-skinned throat, reaching for a chair before I could give him an answer.

"Sure. Come on in and sit down, brother," I said sarcastically.

He bent down gathering his hands up like a steeple. "I have some disturbing news to share with you, Joseph. I pray I'm giving it to you before it gets to your wife." He leaned forward with an incredulous stare.

I shot back a look of concern. "What's up?"

He took a deep breath before allowing his words to escape. "Well, First Lady Joy was talking to her hairstylist earlier today, down there on 2nd Avenue."

"Okay? And?"

"The conversation was all about you."

"Me?"

"She was bragging about…well, I'd rather not give full details of the conversation. But, it was a very graphic and explicit one, to say the least. She also told her stylist that she was supposed to be staying in your Hoover home."

I drew back, trying to play it off. "Was she drunk?"

"Drunk or not, she has started a new rumor mill about what the temporary pastor of Ebenezer has been doing for her."

I cleared my throat, hoping to stay calm. "Continue."

"She kept talking about how she missed you and how lonely she felt living in a hotel without you. How you came to her rescue like you always do and paid for her stay."

"You believe that?"

He gave a skeptical glare. "She also said that you slept with her recently. I thought you were done with that?"

I slapped my hand against my head in disgust. "What did you just say? I haven't slept with that woman since—"

"I don't want to know. My friend called me immediately after she left the salon. I thought you should know."

I felt my eyes burning with humiliation. I looked down at the paperwork and then back at him and said, "Thanks, bro."

His surprised look vanished as sorrow filled his eyes. I was baffled. I realized no matter how much I catered to her nonsense on behalf of Bishop, she still wouldn't let up and did everything to sabotage my life.

"My wife can't handle anymore, bro. She put me out, and if she hears this, I won't be able to come back," I blurted in defense.

He shook his head and responded back, crouching down lower in his seat. "So, what's the plan?"

I leaned back, folding my arms, feeling annoyed. "Only God knows."

He looked up with seriousness in his eyes. I drew back, wishing I could end this conversation. I stood up, abruptly rushing out of the office door, knowing that Timothy would never tell me something if he didn't already investigate it first. I turned around once I ran out the door said, "Thanks, Timothy. I need to get home and check on my wife."

He nodded, following right behind me. "Good idea."

I turned back around to face him. "Keep this to yourself and please, if you hear of anything else, let me know."

"I got you, bruh." He shook my hand.

We marched in step out of the building as we parted ways. I had to get to my wife before this rumor got out. This was the last thing she needed to hear.

CHAPTER 29-JOSEPH

I was only eighteen and didn't know what to expect of an older woman touching my chest. She wrestled me into submission shortly after. Before I knew it, I was meeting her whenever she called for me. The word "freak" didn't fully describe her high sex drive.

"Listen, Joy. This is the end of the road for us. I can't do this anymore."

She licked her lips. "I know how to get to Tuskegee."

"No, what I'm saying is we can't do this anymore. Ever."

She nudged up closer, pushing me into the office desk. "Stop fighting it, handsome. You love it just as much as I do," she said, thrusting her body into mine.

"This is wrong, Joy. Stop it." I mushed her face in the other direction as she poked her lips at me.

She stepped back and rubbed up and down on her thighs. "That's not what you said last night, papi."

I moved away. "Don't call me that."

"Don't be such a little brat. Play along or do you like Cowboys and Indians then?" She giggled, giving a sly grin.

It wasn't long before I found myself falling deeper and deeper for her spell.

"You okay?" the nurse asked

"Uh, yeah."

"Okay, well you can now take Mr. Shackleford home."

I cheesed. I was happy Bishop could finally go home. He still had a long road to recovery, but he was almost there. The nurse's aide pushed him down the hall in a wheelchair. He had a trash bag full of items placed on his lap.

"Hello there, son."

I reached down to hug him. "Bishop, I am so glad to see your face."

"Glad to be amongst the living, son."

"You all set and ready to go?"

"Yes, Lord. There are too many old folks around this place. I need to get around people my age."

We both laughed as he scratched his full gray beard.

I thanked the nurse's aide and pushed him towards the elevator. "Are your children home to greet you?"

"All five of them. They called me this morning. Robert said they were giving me some type of welcome home party or something. You know these young folks love spending my money."

I chuckled. "That's what they are supposed to do, Bishop. You are the man and they know you got it like that."

He smacked his cheek. "Yeah, I bet I ain't got one dollar in my account after that crazy Joy cleared me out."

When we got to the first floor, we headed towards the car. The revolving door twirled us to the outside of the hospital. We laughed and joked about the good times. When we got halfway down the walkway, Joy appeared.

"The woman that wanted to kill her husband has the nerve to show up again. Why are you here, Joy?" Bishop yelled.

She cleared her throat, looking as if she hadn't had a full course meal in weeks. "We're going home."

"We?" he inquired. "You ain't going nowhere with me, woman. Joseph, move forward please." He pointed straight ahead.

She stumbled behind us. "Wait. Michael, I don't have anywhere to stay."

"And?"

I continued to push.

"Don't be like that, baby. You gonna let me live out here like this?"

"Joy, if you don't back up, I will get security out here. Now step aside," he demanded.

She looked at me with sad eyes. She was nonverbally asking me for help.

I didn't say a word as I continued to roll Bishop forward. She stood still in the same spot we left her in. "You all are going to be sorry on how you treated me, both of you."

I got nervous, hoping that this wouldn't be the moment that she started to confess her wrongdoings with me.

"What the heck she talking about, Joseph?" Bishop looked up with fiery eyes.

"I have no idea, Bishop. Let me get you in this car and take you home. You focus on your health. God will have to take care of Joy for you."

"I know that's right. If someone would have warned me, I would've stayed far away from the woman. Beautiful women ain't always what you need, son. Sometimes beauty will kill you before ugly will."

We burst into laughter as I loaded everything in the car. He held onto my arm, scooting in the front seat. I folded up his wheel chair and packed it in the trunk. When I got in the car, he turned to me and said, "Son, you're alright with me. Now, let's hurry up so we can get some of this good ole cake the children got for me. Thank God, I'm finally going home!"

CHAPTER 30-JOY

I twirled the gun around with my index finger several times. It was a lightweight .22 that I bought years ago and kept hidden in the spare tire section of my 1996 Ford Mustang. Although I bought the gun for safety reasons, I now could use it for handling business. Thoughts of taking Joseph and Michael out for mistreatment repeated in my head. I twirled the gun again, pointing to several objects in the room. I imagined myself being a sharp shooter and taking no prisoners.

Was I losing it?

It was nothing that a tall glass of Hennessy or some scotch on the rocks couldn't handle. My mind was going in circles as I thought about feeling lonely. I even thought about finding Scott, the man I slept with that night in the hotel room. Maybe he could help to ease the pain. I took the gun and slowly rubbed it down my legs, exhaling deeply.

Evil thoughts.

Why couldn't I just take Joseph to a foreign land and force him to be my husband?

Why should I have to pull a gun on him to make him act right?

I know he loved me, so why was he fighting it?

I ogled down at the gun, feeling that I had the power to achieve several wishes that came to mind. Or maybe I could kill his wife. After all, that would be due diligence for what she has taken from me. I wasn't afraid of doing any of these things. I didn't believe there was a God anymore. He couldn't possibly be real if he allowed me to suffer like this. I was going to use an extreme measure to get all of their attention. Since no one wanted to play by my rules, I had a trick for all of them.

Click. Click.

I laughed.

I nudged myself upside my forehead with the tip of the gun, remembering to load the bullets. Every piece of metal that slid in the chamber thrilled me. I then moved slowly around the hotel room, holding the gun in one hand while putting pieces of clothing into my suitcase with the other. This was the last and final night of my hotel stay, so I needed to leave for the homeless shelter. I was notified bright and early that morning that I had used the last free night that Joseph paid for. It was the inevitable since he cut me off and I needed to check out by 3 p.m. I didn't have a plan. I tucked the gun in my purse and rolled my suitcase out the door.

"Ma'am, you dropped something." I peeped around the corner at the stranger's voice behind me.

He picked up my old checkbook that fell out of my purse. "Thanks," I said, looking at his big puffy coat that consumed him.

"Are you staying here at the hotel tonight?" he asked as his blue eyes sparkled down at me. He was a tall, slender white man with curly hair. He put me in the mind of a white pimp seen on television that roamed around the hotel to make sure his women were working. He had on everything name brand as his pants hung low below his waist.

"No, this is my last night here. I'm on my way to a homeless shelter."

"A homeless shelter? You are too darn sexy not to be taken care of by someone. Who you with?"

I blinked. "No one." Saying that out loud resonated deeply. "Listen, I will give you a one-hundred-dollar bill if you stay with me tonight."

"Why would you want to do that?" I asked bashfully.

"Of course, it's your payment for spending some time with me."

"I'm not a call girl or anything like that," I huffed, feeling insulted.

"It doesn't matter. You help me and I will help you."

Was that the twenty-first century way of paying for sex? I looked down, wishing my life didn't have to resort to such measures. But, I needed every bit of that money he had to offer. I needed to haggle as much as possible in order to survive.

"Oh, by the way, what's your name?" he asked, rubbing my cheek.

"Joy."

He licked his lips. "Ms. Joy, how about you come back inside and give me all the *joy* I need. I've never been with a black woman before, but I sure do want a piece of you, shugga mama."

I stuck out my hand, demanding the money. "Pay me my money first."

He stared down at my chest. "Sure, sweet thing." He pulled out the crisp one-hundred-dollar bill and handed it to me.

Is this really my life?

I never thought I would have to stoop so low. I was going to do as asked to at least have money to eat with. But, as soon as I finished handling my business, someone was going to be punished for leaving me to die. I didn't appreciate fulfilling this white man's sick fantasy, but I had no other choice.

Two hours later...

I got dressed. It didn't take me long to throw on a tight-fitting skirt and blouse. I smeared on some lipstick around my lips and puckered in the mirror. I looked back at the bed in disgust. That was the worst sex I had ever had. While the white man was fast asleep, I was going to tip out and create a plan to get everyone back that wronged me. Then, after it was all said and done, Joseph would waltz with me into the sunset.

I had to get Selina away from her home so we could have some "girl" talk. That was the first part of my plan. To feed her information that would break her in half. I wanted her to feel my pain, even if I had to tell a few lies. Maybe I could tell her I was pregnant. Probably wouldn't work since I surpassed menopause. I looked young, but everyone knew that I wasn't. I wanted to see her cry first. I wanted her face to be bloodied with tears. Then once I finished with her, I could plant more seeds into the others.

I pulled out my cellphone and dialed her number. "Hello? Selina. Sorry to bother you, but we need to meet for a little chat. I know it's been awhile since we've chatted, but I think there is something very important that you should know."

Within minutes, she had given me an address to a secluded location. I wasn't sure if it would be smart to go to a place that I had never been before when I was trying to do something mischievous.

"What is this about, Joy?"

"I actually have something to give you. It's for the new baby. I promise no strings attached and no games."

She hesitated. "Ok."

"Ok great. Meet me in an hour. I needed to stop by the church first." I had to see Joseph beforehand. I needed to lay eyes on him and tell him how much I loved him. I sat back, just thinking about his touch, his kiss, and his tongue licking my entire body. I shimmered, thinking about all the good times we used to share. Once I made my appearance at Ebenezer's Bible Study, I would take off to handle his naïve wife. It was going to be a busy night for me. I had a lot of things to straighten out in order to have my *man* to myself.

CHAPTER 31-JOSEPH

I was day dreaming as Bible Study was coming to a close. Selina had called me earlier in the day to tell me that she was ready for me to come back home. I was so elated that we could move past everything that happened. I missed my children. I missed my wife.

I looked around the congregation once again for my wife. Selina didn't show up for Bible Study and I had not heard from her stating that she wasn't coming. This wasn't like her. She always attended. I stepped outside to dial her cell number, but I still didn't get a response. Each call was going straight to voicemail. I hastily headed towards the door of the church and in walked Joy Shackleford.

She paused as her eyes locked with mine with a sensual tone. "I miss you."

Luckily, there was no one else in the hallway as most members were still inside. I grabbed her by the arm, shoving her forward and said, "Move on, woman."

She gave a long yawn, not seeming at all surprised that I reacted coldly to her grand entrance. "You must be insane, Joseph. I will never move on."

"You will. You just don't know it yet," I replied sternly.

She put her hand on her hips, smoothing down her expensive silk skirt. "I suggest you get with the program, sweetness."

I was blown away. I couldn't believe she would show up at the church after all that had been said and done. She just wasn't going to give up the ghost of our past. She yanked my face close to hers. "No one is looking...kiss me." She stepped forward and forcefully pushed her lips into mine.

I moved back and wiped my lips clean. "Are you crazy?" I looked around to make sure no one was watching.

"I don't know why you keep playing this faithful role. You want this. You want all of this." She pointed to her private parts.

"You really need to get a grip, Joy. I will say this..." I smirked deviously. "Thank you for helping me focus solely on my wife. The more you push up on me, the more I love her. So, thank you for being a true-blue *stalker*. You have helped my marriage tremendously." I walked off, strutting like I had just won the man of the year award. I hit the church steps as she roared past me.

"There will be a surprise for you when you get home." The silhouette of her body flashed in front of me as I looked in wonder.

"Yes, I know and she is called my lovely and beautiful wife. She is waiting for her husband's return. Now go away."
My strut continued straight to my car. I was yearning to see my wife, hold her tightly, and tell her how much I loved her. I was stronger than ever before and happy that I could resist Joy so easily. Her kiss didn't affect me nor did her words move me.

All of a sudden, I heard a loud screeching noise in front of me. Joy had taken out a switchblade and used it like a pencil to write on the side of my car. I stopped dead in my tracks in shock as the paint chipped away while she formulated big letters. She giggled and twirled each letter in cursive.

"Oh, my God. Why are you doing this?"

She didn't stop, nor did she look up to respond. I ran up to her and tried to push her away, but it was too late. When she finished her cursive masterpiece, the words *Joy's Man for Life* was written across the passenger side door. She stood up proud with her hands on her hips as she pointed to her artwork.

"You like it?" she asked, while breathing heavily.

I was ready to bum rush her, but church members started walking out of the building. They moved quickly to see what all the ruckus was about as they responded to my howling.

Unfortunately, I was exposed. If they didn't know about me and Joy before, they definitely knew all about us now. I cried, covering my face completely. The shame and hurt that I never wanted to face in front of my church members had finally reared its ugly face, smack dab in the church parking lot.

She spat, "Never forget who you belong to, Joseph." She marched to her car, holding the switch blade in the air. She then reached inside her car and grabbed a gun. She walked around to the driver's side and aimed close range to the door. Four shots were fired as bullet holes pierced through the metal. I stood there too embarrassed to turn around and face the others. I was going to be the laughingstock as I heard a few giggles, along with some ahhs and oohs behind me. Joy blew the smoke from the tip of her gun and trotted to her car. Every muscle in my body screamed as I wanted to do something foul to her. But, all eyes were on me and I had to remain composed. I was torn inside. The agony of watching someone I used to love destroy my prized possession, my two-door sports car, made me ache. I looked back as some of the church members had their arms folded and their faces scrunched. My squeaky-clean reputation was tarnished, thanks to Joy.

CHAPTER 32-SELINA

It was so cold outside but yet I waited patiently. I was anxious to see what Joy had for the kids as I had forgiven her for all her wrongdoing. Since the Weeping River was the place where I forgave many, I didn't mind talking to her there. I felt it was the safest place since God's anointing was all over it. Minutes seemed like hours as I sat at the edge of the river bank, enjoying the night air. I watched attentively as people walked back and forth to the restaurant for their last and final moments of enjoyment before closing time. I was hoping whatever gift she had for the children wouldn't require a long, drawn-out conversation to go with it. Don't know how I forgave her to get to this point, but I did.

I was ready to see Joseph. I missed him.

As I looked down at my watch and then back at the river, I couldn't help but wonder if Joy was really going to meet me as planned. I don't know why I trusted her to be on time. She wasn't on time for anything. A Ford Mustang pulled up and circled around the property a few times before parking directly in front of me. The car's bright headlights shined on my back as I stood up tall. I tried to view the driver, but it was too dark to see anything. I wasn't familiar with the car as I remembered Joy driving a red Jeep Cherokee when she came to church. But, I didn't know who else would be out here in this dark area this late at night, considering the restaurant took its last customer thirty minutes prior.

The car didn't move. The driver didn't get out and I couldn't see anything past the tinted windows. I waved, hoping to get some form of response from whomever was behind the wheel. But, I got nothing.

"Is someone there? Is that you, Joy?" I said as my voice echoed.

The engine revved several times. I looked around to see who else witnessed this mysterious car just sitting there. The workers of the restaurant were cleaning up and weren't paying attention to the activities outside the restaurant.

"Hello?" I wanted to move closer. Instead, I put my head down for a split second and before I knew it, I felt a sharp pain gush through my intestines. Apparently, the unidentified car rammed into me without warning. My body was thrown into the weeping river by force of the heavy metal machine. I felt a big splash as my body hit the cold water instantly. The muddy water floated down my throat. I couldn't swim, and even if I could, my ribs felt shattered from the impact as I held my chest tightly. Every now and again, I floated to the top, gasping for air and swallowing water. I thought to myself, *God, please don't take me away from my children. They need me more than anyone. Don't allow them to lose me like I lost my parents.* I gargled the murky water like Listerine. Then, I bobbed up and down, trying to swim using the butterfly method that I attempted to learn as a child in summer camp. Several small items were hitting the water quickly. It was bullets hitting the surface and trickling down to the deep. A tide of water shifted me. It was as if God maneuvered my body to miss each and every gun-smoke-filled item that emerged into the water.

Thank you, God.

The question why was asked over and over again in my mind. Why would someone try to hurt me? I could faintly hear the car skidding across the parking lot and getting away. I could also hear screams from the workers and customers as a few jumped into the water to rescue me. God's voice was clear as a whistle: *Overcomers never quit. Quitters never overcome. Don't quit, child.*

I was shivering profusely as the icy waters numbed my hands and feet. A young waiter with his waiter's robe on, grabbed my hand and threw a floating device in front of me. He pulled the device sideways as my body clung to it tightly. He directed me to the bank of the river. I could only see shadows as my eyes were filled with mud and debris. I could not see faces.

"Ma'am. Breathe," he said, standing over me positioning his lips to give me mouth to mouth.

Could this be the beginning of my end?

I closed my eyes as I heard someone scream, "Oh, my God, I think she's dying."

CHAPTER 33-JOSEPH

I sat in the recliner after arriving at the Hoover home. I was in deep thought. My car was ruined, and after having that kind of graffiti attached to it, I couldn't drive it anywhere. I was still teary-eyed. I tried to reflect on where I went wrong with Joy. I guess fulfilling her request for sex was going to be a lifelong consequence. I couldn't get over all the stares from God's people while in the parking lot. All the whispers around me made me want to run and hide. I'm sure the respect they had for me oozed out of their bodies while they snickered in awe. I called Selina's cell several times. No matter how mad she would be, she never missed Bible study. I was now very concerned. As I tried to compose my thoughts, I felt sleepy. Suddenly, I drifted.

"Joseph! Stop running from me!"

"I don't call it running, Ms. Joy. I just don't think getting in between the sheets with a church member is what I should be doing at my age."

Her eyes grew large as she shoved me against the hotel door. This time, she wanted to spend more than a few minutes with me. She wanted to lay beside me all night. I was only twenty-four hours away from my departure to Tuskegee University. I wanted to hurry up and leave Hoover to get away from all the madness.

Her long lashes fluttered as she gave me an intense look, pushing me into the room. I tried to be tough, but she broke me down once again. I was now enthralled by her smell, enticed by her touch, and captured by her beauty. She was my master and I was her slave.

As she grabbed my crotch tightly, I throbbed all over. She craned her neck to reach my lips as my fingers ran through her tresses. Although it was wrong, it felt so right. We didn't have to use any words to state our wants and needs. Our hands and eyes did all the talking for us. I cuffed her backside closer to me after giving in to her wicked spell. I was mystified. She pinned the heel of her shoe on the chair beside us while I moaned for more. When it was all over, she laid on the bed in silence. I closed my eyes, turning towards the wall. I was disgusted with myself once again. Tears spilled onto the sheets as shame filled my heart. I frantically wiped my tears away while she snored loudly. This was not how I wanted to spend my last day of freedom in my hometown before going off to college.

My mother would probably lay hands on me if she ever found out about our indiscretions. I'm sure my father would be proud. But for me, it was the most disgraceful time of my life.

I heard the security alarm being turned off. The nanny entered the room as I felt her presence standing over me.

"How you feeling, Mr. Witherspoon?"

"Okay, I guess."

"Is Ms. Selina coming home soon?"

"I don't know. You haven't seen her either?"

She looked puzzled. "No, sir."

I pulled up from the seat.

"Have you called the house in Atlanta? Maybe she forgot something for the kids."

"Yes, sir, I did."

The nanny's hands twitched. "Something is wrong, Mr. Joseph. I feel it. I just got a funny feeling that something has gone terribly wrong."

I grabbed my coat quickly. I was going to search for my wife, even if it took all night to find her. I jumped in the car and looked up at the sky. "Lord, please bring my wife home. She is all I have, Lord. Everything I worked hard for is now ruined. I deserve it all, but I just want my wife." I immediately called my parents' house as I jumped in the family van.

"Ma, have you seen Selina today?"

"No, I haven't. What's wrong, son?"

"Ma, now is not the time for twenty-one questions."

"I got a call from Sister Emma already, telling me about what happened to your car. Are you okay, son?"

"Ma, please. I don't want to talk about that. That's the least of my worries. I'm looking for my wife."

"I haven't seen her. Why isn't she home this time of night?"

I shouted in panic. "If I knew I wouldn't be calling, *Mama*. I'm desperately looking for her. Please call the other sisters and see if they've seen her."

"You better look hard, son. You better hope she comes back to you. You have put that woman through enough and it's time out for playin' with her and God."

"No more games, Mama. I love her. I love her more now than ever before. I realized how much she means to me. I just want things to be the way they used to be, that's all. I want her to be the woman I met at school. I want her to love me the way she used to."

I could tell my mother was giving a smile of love through the phone as her tone changed. "I'm going to pray that things get back to the good old days. You two make a cute couple. But learn to keep your eyes on heaven, son, and not on other women. Trouble don't last always."

I smirked. My mother was right. I wish I could fit through the phone and lean into her chest for a hug. There was nothing like a mother's love. There was nothing like the love of a wife either.

One hour later…

I circled around all of downtown Birmingham. I went back home, weeping heavily as I parked the van and ran inside. Selina was still not home. Within seconds, Jessica walked into the room, crying loudly.

"What's wrong, honey?" I reached for her curly locks and rubbed her hair down.

"Mommy. Where's Mommy?"

"What do you mean, where is Mommy?"

She pointed with her little finger toward the door.

I tiptoed down the stairs, holding my baby girl in my arms. "I'm sure she's downstairs making a sandwich, baby girl." After stepping off the last step, no Selina. I searched the entire house.

I went into the kitchen, asking the nanny once again, "Ms. Willow, have you heard from Selina yet?"

"No, sir." She was startled that Selina wasn't found.

I rubbed my face, feeling drained. This was not like Selina at all. There were only two things I could think of at the moment: she was either too depressed to come home, or she was somewhere asleep enjoying her peace. But, it was way past her normal time of arrival and it wasn't like her to not check in on the kids. I'm sure she was at the private spot she always talked about. Lately, she spent most of her time there, then at home. She never gave me the name of the location, but she did inform me that it was a great place to visit and that Timothy suggested it. If nothing else, Timothy would have the information needed to find her.

I picked up the phone next to the nightstand to call him. "Yooo, bruh. Where is the place that Selina goes every day? She hasn't been home yet."

"Bruh, it's past midnight. What do you mean? That place shuts down at eleven thirty p.m. nightly."

"She's not here, bro, and I'm trying not to go off on the deep end but this is so strange, man."

"Okay, here is the address. 2646 Longley Road. It's not too far from Leeds, I will meet you there."

The next thing I knew, I was headed down a winding road, full of trees and deer running against the wind on each side. I didn't know where I was going but I hoped and prayed that when I arrived, Selina would be sitting on the edge of the water journaling with a flashlight in front of her or reading her favorite book.

CHAPTER 34-JOSEPH

I felt a choking feeling around my neck. My wife was laying on the ground when I arrived, with paramedics surrounding her. Blood was gushing from her head and onto the embankment. I was hysterical. I didn't know what to do. Timothy had arrived before me and plopped down to the ground, crying harder than I did. "Oh, my God. Oh, my God." I spun around in confusion, not knowing what to do next. Did postpartum drive Selina into trying to take her own life? Was she stressed out that bad from being a mother, to the point where she had to leave us like this?

I sat down on the cold and muddy ground next to Timothy full of anguish. The paramedics moved her body onto the stretcher. I felt dizzy as if I was fainting. "Oh no, Selina. Oh no." I held my head and cried some more.

All the dreams and hopes of giving her everything she was denied were gone. I owed her for all the things I did to make her unhappy. I was planning to make it all up to her one day. But, as I looked over, she seemed lifeless. She had foam around her mouth and discolored lips. I tried to control my emotions.

"What did I miss, bro? What did I miss? She seemed to be getting better."

"Selina, why would you do this? Why would you want to leave those babies?" Timothy yelled as if she was going to answer back.

A man from the restaurant came over to explain what had happened. "Are you the victim's husband?"

"Yes," I mumbled.

"There was an accident. A car that looked like a mustang came onto the lot and did this."

"What did the car look like?" Timothy inquired.

"I think it was an old Ford Mustang. The person driving it revved up their engine a few times and then came rushing out of nowhere toward the young lady."

"What!" I braced myself as he continued.

"The impact of the car pushed her into the water. A few of the workers jumped in and threw floatation devices in the water to try and save her. She sucked in a lot of water, so I'm sure she has some form of hypothermia."

"A Mustang?" I looked over at Timothy.

"Yeah, gray-looking…older model."

Joy…

I became belligerent as tears rolled down my crimson sweater.

"She's breathing. Let's take her in," a paramedic replied. They rushed across the muddy walkway with the stretcher lifted up high above the ground. I jumped in the back of the ambulance and grabbed her hand, hoping to feel a pulse or see her eyes open to notice me.

"Come on, baby. Come on, don't leave me like this."

Timothy followed behind me, still crying loudly. "I'm going to follow the ambulance." He screamed in frustration. "Did Joy do this, bro? Did she?" He was devastated. "I told you to leave that woman alone. I told you she was dangerous. That's my little sister, bro. She don't deserve this, man." He jumped up and down like a child having a tantrum, before exiting to his car.

I wanted to bang my head up against something hard. I would rather hurt and take the pain, than to see Selina like this. The stillness of Selina's body terrified me as her breathing was minimal.

Why did I get back involved with a woman I knew was no good?

Why did I allow sin to consume me?

I had reaped what I sowed and now my baby girl was fighting for her life, due to my transgressions. This had to be a bad dream. Something awful began to formulate in my head. I wanted to hurt Joy with my bare hands. I had to shake the thoughts away. Because if I find her, this would surely be Joy's last day residing in this place called Earth.

CHAPTER 35-JOY

I rushed from the scene, breathing hard and heavy driving over eighty miles per hour. I wasn't expecting all of that to happen as adrenaline pumped up and down my chest. My initial plan was just to scare her. I thought if I just tapped her a little bit with the car, she would beg for mercy. I didn't realize she was that close to the water, therefore falling completely in.

How did I lose control like that?

I envisioned having photos of me and Joseph, posing together on an exotic island and living happily ever after. We would have a destination wedding, where only his children were invited. In spite of all my wrongdoing, I still wanted him badly. Maybe getting rid of his wife would be beneficial after all in the grand scheme of things.

"Oh, my God, Joseph?" I covered my mouth, talking to myself after coming to the realization of how much this would hurt him. Where was I going to go now? Who would believe me if I told them this was all an accident? Maybe I could give a fake mental health diagnosis if I got caught for doing all of this. There was no doubt that Timothy sicced the police squad on me. The only crime I committed was a crime of passion. Could I go to jail for loving someone way too much? I'm sure everyone was looking for me throughout the entire city.

"Lord, what am I going to do now?" I pressed against the stirring wheel.

My face felt like it was sizzling from the heat of my heavy breathing in the car. My nose started to bleed from all the excitement as blood dripped onto my sleeves. It suddenly came to me that if I left the bloody shirt in the car and found other transportation, maybe I could fool everyone into thinking I was dead. I drove back to the hotel to find the man I'd tricked with. His car was still in the parking lot. Maybe he could help me get out of all this. When I got out and knocked on the door, he swung the door open widely and said, "Are you back for more?" giving a sarcastic grin.

"I did something terribly wrong. I need your help."

He looked at me with a peculiar glare. "Come on in."

I spent over thirty minutes giving him all the details of what happened. He seemed to find humor in some parts as he inched over to put his arm around me.

"So, it looks like you need me, huh, sweetness?"

I cringed. I didn't want to be dependent on a white pimp but he was all I had for now. "I need to hide out somewhere. Can you help me?"

"Yes. I got a house full of girls in Anniston that I can let you stay in. Girls of all ages are living there. I think you would be a good mother figure to some of them. Maybe you can even show them the ropes."

"The ropes?'

"We need more experienced women like you on our team. With a body like yours, we can make a killing in this industry."

I felt so insulted, but what could I possibly say after taking his cash for sex? I had to shake it off and do what needed to be done in order to remain free. I pulled off my bloody shirt and replaced it with an Alabama State T-shirt he had laying on the hotel chair. I then walked to the car and placed the bloody shirt inside as my decoy.

He walked behind me steadily and asked, "You ready?"

I nodded reluctantly.

"Don't look so sad, mama. This could be a new beginning for you. For everything there is a season and this is your season to make some serious money." He chuckled as we walked to his pick-up truck.

Prostitution? A whore house? From a first lady to a call girl?
I felt sick to my stomach. If I'd stayed in God's will, things would be different. I betrayed the first man that ever really loved me for this? I couldn't think straight.

"So, where you from?" he asked.

"I'm from Birmingham, born and raised. I forgot to ask...what's your name?" I looked over, misty-eyed.

"James, but most people call me Jimmy."

"Thanks for your help, Jimmy." I started fidgeting my hands. I probably could've just shot him with my gun pressed down in my purse and took his vehicle, but it wouldn't fix my money problems, so I had to go along with the entire scheme. I was in a daze as we floated down Highway 20.

Then he asked, "What was your occupation before you got into this line of work, honey?"

I paused and answered reluctantly. "Once upon a time, I used to be the first lady of a well-known church in the area. That was my occupation."

He laughed hysterically. "You're joking, right?"

"No, sir, I'm not."

He looked over and smirked. "All I know about religion is that God blesses the child that has it's own. It's time to get your own, honey. You got what it takes to be the queen of my establishment. So, let's go make this money, shall we?"

I was numb. I wanted to go home...wherever that might be.

CHAPTER 36-JOSEPH

Two weeks later...

Selina came home with only a few bumps and bruises from the accident. I was glad to have her back in my arms and with the children. She walked with a limp around the house and moved slowly. But the good thing was she was alive. I never realized how much she meant to me until this tragedy. I appreciated her so much now. She endured a lot dealing with a man like me over the last few years. I wanted to erase it all and start over from the beginning of our love story.

We sat on the living room couch, watching the children play hide and go seek around the room. They had grown so much right before our eyes. I put my arms around Selina and held her tightly. I didn't want to let her go. She put her hand on my knee and rubbed it with care. I didn't know what I could say to make her feel better about this entire ordeal. But, I knew my actions would speak volumes over my actual words. So instead of saying anything, I just sat and enjoyed the moment of holding her close in my arms.

I wondered what happened to Joy. I also wondered if

Timothy had the mob squad hunting her down like a blood hound by now. I realized quickly that everything that looks green on the other side has a different color once you walk up on it. I felt so convicted for doing my baby girl like this. I also felt so used by Joy. I felt bad about it all.

"Hey, honey? Let's all go out and get something to eat. It's been awhile since we did something with all of the children. Are you up to eating out tonight?" I asked with sincerity.

She paused and whispered slowly, "I forgive you."

I doubled back not expecting that response. "Huh?"

"I forgive you, Joseph. I sat in that hospital bed saying to myself that God gave us these trials and tribulations for us to become a power couple. I don't blame you for anything. After all, Joy was a very manipulative woman. Being that she was your first, you felt you had a permanent soul tie with her. I understand that now."

I looked away, ashamed. "Yeah, I guess you're right. Thank you."

"God always makes a way, Joseph. He still provided protection even in the midst of our storm. He showed us what love is all about through this ordeal. So with that, I will say again, I forgive you."

I sucked up my tears. I wanted to cry but not because I was sad. I wanted to cry tears of happiness. The fact that my wife could be so kind-hearted to me after all that had been said and done. She truly had a heart of gold.

"Selina, I want to make it all up to you. How can I make this go away?"

She looked over and smiled. "I just want you to love God with all of your heart. When you love Him, you will be able to truly love me. Now that's how a husband learns to love his wife…through God."

I kissed her on the cheek and helped her off the couch. When we stood up, I hugged her tightly and kissed her on the neck. "Now, let's go get something to eat."

The children jumped around, cheering when they heard the word eat. They were always excited about going out for dinner as it was a rare occasion for us. They were rambunctious to say the least but I finally got a chance to not only enjoy my children, I also finally had time to enjoy my wife. Bishop was back in his rightful place, the pulpit. Ebenezer carried on fine without me. I gladly gave all of his duties back to him. I thought I was ready to be the next mega ministry preacher, but then I realized I might want to work on how to be a wonderful husband first. God gave us a second chance and I was going to cherish every moment I had with my wife and kids.

CHAPTER 37-TIMOTHY

"Stand down!" my partner yelled with a raspy voice that escaped from behind the Ford Mustang that was parked in front of Motel 6. My goal was to shoot her dead and ask questions later. But when I got closer to what I thought was a body sitting up straight in the car, I realized Joy had tricked us. She had taken a few pillows and stood them up straight with a bloody shirt over them.

"Ugh!"

"Calm down, son." My partner's name was Lawson. He was a few months close to retirement and he was nowhere near trigger happy like me. When it came to hurting those I cared about, I would go to war.

"I'm not calming down until I find her."

"She's probably long gone by now, son."

"You're probably right, but that doesn't stop me from trying."

He gave a sorrowful exchange with pleading hands. "Let it go. Your friend is back home and she's safe. Don't allow yourself to seek revenge to the point where you want to kill someone. Do the right thing, son."

"Yea, she probably isn't worth the bullets in this revolver." I patted my gun down towards my side.

We stood there trying to figure out what to do next, as a young lady came out of one of the rooms walking towards the Mustang. When she looked up and saw us standing there, she turned back around hurriedly to go back inside.

"Wait. Stop right there!"

She stopped dead in her tracks facing the other direction.

"Do you know the owner of this car young lady?" I walked around to the other side to see her face.

"No, sir, I don't," she trembled. She was a young girl with long blonde hair that extended to the middle of her back. She had chipped teeth and seemed to have missed several meals as her bony body wavered.

"Don't lie, please. Looks like we might have to take you in to get the truth out of you." I pointed in her face.

"Please. Please I'm out here doing this for my family. I need the money he gives me. Please don't do this."

I put my hand on my chin and asked, "So, how do you make your money, young lady? Who is he?"

She put her head down and mumbled, "Sir, please, don't make me tell you. This is the only way my family can eat and if I snitch, he's going to kill me."

"How old are you?" Lawson asked, bewildered to see such a young child doing grown folks' business.

"Fourteen," she said, putting her head down.

I looked over with disgust. "I won't bother you, if you tell me where the owner of this car is."

"I don't know. I was just told by Jimmy to come out here and drive it around the corner to this empty parking lot."

"Jimmy? Is that your—"

"Sir, please." She put her hand up to her mouth.

"Okay, I'm sorry, no more questions." I gave her my card. "But if you hear anything, or you find yourself up to telling me, please call me."

She nodded.

"Sad situation, isn't it?" Lawson walked slowly to the car in deep thought.

"Unfortunately, I see this all the time on these streets. Let's go home and try this again tomorrow. I got to find out who this Jimmy guy is that she spoke of. I'm sure he will lead me right to Joy."

CHAPTER 38-SELINA

It was Sunday morning and it was Joseph's turn to give a word. I sat up close to the pulpit, smiling proudly at my husband. He wore a purple and gold robe that made his skin tone shimmer in the light. I couldn't believe that we were back to being the normal couple we used to be, without any worries or melodrama lingering in our lives. I always wondered where Joy could be, or if she was even alive for that matter. I prayed that Timothy hadn't found her and buried her in some ditch deep in the country. But, nevertheless, as long as she stayed far away from me and my family, all was well with the world.

Bishop was still not a hundred percent to return as all of the congregation had thought. Joseph continued off and on as the speaker, until Bishop felt up to preaching again. Thankfully, the congregation still received him with open arms in spite of all the rumors that had circulated about Joseph's stalker experience.

"Lift your hands up and tell God thank you. I said, lift your hands up and tell God thank you, church!" Joseph was on fire this morning and the congregation rolled right along with him. He had grown so much since the accident and he was truly a man after God's own heart.

Before he started his sermon, he said, "I give an honor to God and to the Bishop of this house." Then, he paused and looked over at me on the first row. "But, I especially give honor to my beautiful wife. She is my everything, y'all." The crowd was touched by his sentiment as I blew him a kiss at his kind words. God gave us a new beginning and although we had a few delayed moments, we were no longer denied unconditional love. I loved *us* as a family unit and I now loved being the wife of Minister Joseph Witherspoon. We didn't give up and because of our endurance, God gave us the strength we needed to overcome.

EPILOGUE

After an hour of driving, Jimmy stopped at a gas station to get some snacks. I hadn't eaten all day and felt like chewing my fingernails off. He was cheesing the entire time as if he had found his permanent money maker. When he re-entered the car, he was holding a tall bag of food and a few fruit punch drinks.

"You alright over there, pretty lady?"

"Yes," I answered abruptly, flapping my arms.

"Now that we have only thirty minutes left of our drive, I need to put this blindfold on you."

"What?" I looked back surprised.

He reached in his pocket, pulling the blindfold out. "Yes, none of the girls know how to get to any of my houses. I have three hidden in Anniston. All they have is the city location."

"But you just said I was going to be the queen."

He blinked as if he forgot what he said. "Maybe one day, if you show some kind of loyalty to the game, you can pick up girls from Birmingham and bring them to Anniston without me. But for now, you got to let me put this over your eyes."

I moved away as he moved closer.

"Now listen, I don't need you resisting nothing, ya hear? I need you to behave and do what you're told. You've been doing good so far."

I was frantic as his hands rifled the blindfold around my head.

"Now, that's better. When you get used to this kind of life, you will thank me later for being so cautious."

Within seconds, the blindfold was soaked. I couldn't stop crying. I'd lost everything for this? I ran over someone's wife to fulfill a void? I became sad. I began to recollect and regret all of my actions. Then, hate filled the open space in my heart. I hated Joseph for not wanting me. I hated Michael for not being Joseph. I hated Selina for being Joseph's wife. I hated anything and everything.

As I sat quietly, replaying everything over and over in my head, I discovered I still felt the need to have some form of revenge. I wanted to get everyone back for not allowing me to have my ultimate prize, Joseph.

Suddenly, I thought about what Bishop used to always say to me when I was tempted to go back to drinking. I could hear him clearly in my head, "Joy, don't worry about it, pray about it. As a matter of fact, pray until something happens."

This was a desperate time for me and it called for desperate measures. I practiced praying for everyone else while at Ebenezer, but somehow I seemed to forget how to pray for myself. I leaned my head back on the head rest and started praying silently like never before.

ABOUT THE AUTHOR

Teresa B. Howell

Teresa B. Howell was raised in Boston, Massachusetts. She is an educator, mentor, and advocate for students with special needs. Born and raised in the church, it was fitting to tell her story in her unique style of writing. She currently resides in Durham, North Carolina with her husband and children.

That Church Life 1, 2 & 3 is available on Amazon.com and Barnesandnoble.com.

For more information or updates:
www.teresabhowell.com